WITHDRAWN

ALDOUS HUXLEY

The Doors of Perception
and
Heaven and Hell

With a foreword by
J. G. Ballard

and a biographical introduction by
David Bradshaw

Flamingo
An Imprint of HarperCollins*Publishers*

Flamingo
An Imprint of HarperCollins*Publishers*
77–85 Fulham Palace Road,
Hammersmith, London W6 8JB

A Flamingo Modern Classic 1994
16 15 14 13 12 11

Previously published by Grafton 1977
Reprinted 17 times

The Doors of Perception was first published in Great Britain by
Chatto & Windus Ltd 1954
Heaven and Hell was first published in Great Britain by Chatto & Windus Ltd 1956

ISBN 0 00 654731 1

Set in Baskerville

Printed and bound in Great Britain by
Caledonian International Book Manufacturing Ltd, Glasgow

Aldous Huxley

was born on 26 July 1894 near Godalming, Surrey. He began writing poetry and short stories in his early twenties, but it was his first novel, *Crome Yellow* (1921), which established his literary reputation. This was swiftly followed by *Antic Hay* (1923), *Those Barren Leaves* (1925) and *Point Counter Point* (1928) – bright, brilliant satires in which Huxley wittily but ruthlessly passed judgement on the shortcomings of contemporary society. For most of the 1920s Huxley lived in Italy and an account of his experiences there can be found in *Along the Road* (1925).

In the years leading up to the Second World War, Huxley's work took on a more sombre tone in response to the confusion of a society which he felt to be spinning dangerously out of control. The great novels of ideas, including his most famous work *Brave New World* (published in 1932 this warned against the dehumanising aspects of scientific and material 'progress') and the pacifist novel *Eyeless in Gaza* (1936) were accompanied by a series of wise and brilliant essays, collected in volume form under such titles as *Music at Night* (1931) and *Ends and Means* (1937).

In 1937, at the height of his fame, Huxley left Europe to live in California, working for a time as a screenwriter in Hollywood. As the West braced itself for war, Huxley came increasingly to believe that the key to solving the world's problems lay in changing the individual through mystical enlightenment. The exploration of the inner life through mysticism and hallucinogenic drugs was to dominate his work for the rest of his life. His beliefs found expression in both fiction (*Time Must Have A Stop*, 1944 and *Island*, 1962) and non-fiction (*The Perennial Philosophy*, 1945, *Grey Eminence*, 1941 and the famous account of his first mescalin experience, *The Doors of Perception*, 1954).

Huxley died in California on 22 November 1963.

Foreword by J.G. Ballard

If *Brave New World* is Aldous Huxley's greatest novel, then *The Doors of Perception* is his most important work of non-fiction, and I suspect that together they will outlast everything else written by him during his long and restless life. *Brave New World*'s unsettling picture of a scientifically engineered utopia, with its recreational drugs and test-tube babies, its 'feelie' cinemas that anticipate virtual reality, now seems a shrewder guess at the future than George Orwell's vision of Stalinist terror in *Nineteen Eighty-Four*.

Yet *The Doors of Perception* may prove to be even more prophetic than *Brave New World*. All his life Huxley was driven by a need to understand the mystery of human consciousness, a quest that led him from Christian mysticism to the religions of the Far East and the pseudo-religions of California. Unusually for a literary intellectual, of his day or ours, Huxley was intensely interested in science, and much of his original work lies in the border zone between religion, art and science.

The Doors of Perception sits in the centre of this magnetic ground. Huxley was fascinated by early research in the neurosciences, and in particular by the role of neurotransmitters in our brains and the way in which these chemical messengers control our view of ourselves and the world around us. Despite the wonders of human consciousness, Huxley believed that our brains have been trained during the evolutionary millennia to screen out all those perceptions that do not directly aid us in our day to day struggle for existence. We have gained security and survival, but in the process have sacrificed our sense of wonder.

The dismantling of these screens and the revelation of the richer world beyond them has long been the task of art and religious mysticism, but Huxley suspected that modern pharmacology possessed even stronger weapons in its armoury of psycho-active drugs. In *The Doors of Perception* he describes an afternoon in Los Angeles in 1953 when he first ingested mescalin, the active principle of the sacred cactus known to the Mexicans as peyotl, and saw the gates of a new world open before him.

From the start he realised that his insights were not into himself and his modest personal history, but into the universe around him. Over the years there have been endless accounts of mescalin and LSD trips, but none can match Huxley's description of the hallucinatory realm that expanded before his eyes. The shutters around his mind at last fell away, revealing the wonders of existence to his self-centred and earthbound mind.

In *The Doors of Perception* and its sequel, *Heaven and Hell*, Huxley speculates that human beings will always need some sort of chemical aid to free themselves from the inherited limitations of their own nervous systems. Forty years after his mescalin trip beside a Hollywood garden, when we have flown to the moon and girdled our planet with an entertainment culture more suffocating than anything visualised in *Brave New World*, we may be right to think that the expedition Huxley undertook into his own brain is the last journey waiting for all of us, whether by chemical means or through some less hazardous door, the inward passage to our truer and richer selves.

ALDOUS HUXLEY (1894–1963)

On 26 July 1894, near Godalming in Surrey, Aldous Leonard Huxley was born into a family which had only recently become synonymous with the intellectual aristocracy. Huxley's grandfather, Thomas Henry Huxley, had earned notoriety as 'Darwin's bulldog' and fame as a populariser of science, just as his own probing and controversial works were destined to outrage and exhilarate readers and non-readers alike in the following century. Aldous Huxley's mother was a niece of the poet and essayist Matthew Arnold, and he was a nephew of the redoubtable Mrs Humphry Ward, doyenne of late-Victorian novelists. This inheritance, combining the scientific and the literary in a blend which was to become characteristic of his vision as a writer, was both a source of great pride and a burden to Huxley in his formative years. Much was expected of him.

Three traumatic events left their mark on the young Huxley. In 1908 his mother died of cancer, and this led to the effective break-up of the family home. Two years later, while a schoolboy at Eton, Huxley contracted an eye infection which made him almost completely blind for a time and severely impaired his vision for the rest of his life. The suicide of his brother Trevenen in August 1914 robbed Huxley of the person to whom he felt closest. Over twenty years later, in *Eyeless in Gaza* (1936), Huxley's treatment of the death of the main character's mother and his embodiment of 'Trev' in the novel as the vulnerable Brian Foxe give some indication of the indelible pain which these tragic occurrences left in their wake. To a considerable degree, they account for the darkness, pungency and cynicism which feature so prominently in Huxley's work throughout the inter-war period.

Within months of achieving a First in English Language and Literature at Balliol College, Oxford in 1916, Huxley published *The Burning Wheel*, Huxley's first collection of verse, and the three which followed it, *Jonah* (1917), *The Defeat of Youth* (1918) and *Leda* (1920), reveal his indebtedness to French symbolism and *fin de siècle* aestheticism. Also discernible, however, beneath the poetry's triste and ironic patina, is a concern with the inward world of the spirit which anticipates Huxley's later absorption in mysticism. These volumes of poetry were the first of over fifty separate works of fiction, drama, verse, criticism, biography, travel and speculative writing which Huxley was to produce during the course of his life.

Unfit for military service, Huxley worked as a farm labourer at Lady Ottoline Morrell's Garsington Manor after he left Oxford. Here he met not only D.H. Lawrence, Bertrand Russell, Clive Bell, Mark Gertler and other Bloomsbury figures, but also a Belgian refugee, Maria Nys, whom he married in 1919. By then Huxley was working for the *Athenaeum* magazine under the adroit editorship of Middleton Murry. Soon after he became the first British editor of *House and Garden*, worked for *Vogue* and contributed musical criticism to the *Weekly Westminster Gazette* in the early 1920s.

Limbo (1920), a collection of short stories, preceded the appearance of *Crome Yellow* in 1921, the novel with which Huxley first made his name as a writer. Inspired by, among others, Thomas Love Peacock, Norman Douglas and Anatole France, Huxley's first novel incorporated many incidents from his sojourn at Garsington as well as mischevious portraits of its chatelaine and his fellow guests. More blatantly still, *Crome Yellow* is an iconoclastic tilt at the Victorian and Edwardian mores which had resulted in the First World War and its terrible aftermath. For all its comic bravura, which won acclaim from writers such as Scott Fitzgerald and Max Beerbohm, *Crome Yellow* may be read, along with Lytton Strachey's *Eminent Victorians* (1918) and Huxley's second novel *Antic Hay* (1923), as an expression of the pervasive mood of disenchantment in the early 1920s. Huxley told his father that *Antic Hay* was 'written by a member of what I may call the war-generation for others of his kind'. He went on to say that it was intended to reflect 'the life and opinions of an age which has seen the violent disruption of almost all the standards, conventions and values current in the previous epoch'.

Even as a schoolboy Huxley had been an avid browser among the volumes of the *Encyclopaedia Britannica*, and it did not take long for him to acquire a reputation for arcane eclecticism. Moreover, as his prestige as a debunker and an emancipator grew, so Huxley was condemned more roundly by critics of the old guard, such as James Douglas of the *Daily Express*, who denounced the explicit discussion of sex and free thought in his fiction. *Antic Hay* was burned in Cairo, and in the ensuing years many of Huxley's books were censured, censored or banned at one time or another. Conversely, it was the openness, wit, effortless learning and apparent insouciance of Huxley's early work which proved such an appetising concoction for novelists as diverse as Evelyn Waugh, William Faulkner, Anthony Powell and Barbara Pym. Angus Wilson called Huxley 'the god of my adolescence'.

From 1923 onwards Huxley lived abroad more or less permanently, first near Florence and then, between 1930 and 1937, at Sanary on the Côte d'Azur. In *Along the Road* (1925), subtitled 'Notes and Essays of a Tourist', Huxley offered a lively and engaging account of the places and works of art he had taken in since his arrival in Italy, and both the title story of his third collection of tales, *Little Mexican* (1924), and his third novel, *Those Barren Leaves* (1925), are set in that country. According to Huxley, the theme of *Those Barren Leaves* is 'the undercutting of everything by a sort of despairing scepticism and then the undercutting of that by mysticism'. For W.B. Yeats, *Those Barren Leaves* heralded the return of philosophy to the English novel, but it was with his fourth novel, *Point Counter Point* (1928), that Huxley cemented his reputation with the reading public as a thought-provoking writer of fiction. *Point Counter Point* is Huxley's first true 'novel of ideas', the type of fiction with which he has become most closely identified. He once explained that his aim as a novelist was 'to arrive, technically, at a perfect fusion of the novel and the essay', arguing that the novel should be like a holdall, bursting with opinion and arresting ideas. This privileging of content over form was one of the many things he had in common with H.G. Wells; it was anathema to the likes of Virginia Woolf. Huxley was fascinated by the fact that 'the same person is simultaneously a mass of atoms, a physiology, a mind, an object with a shape that can be painted, a cog in the economic machine, a voter, a lover etc', and one of his key aims in *Point Counter Point* was to offer this multi-faceted view of his principal characters.

Huxley's more sombre mood in the late 1920s was epitomised by *Proper Studies* (1927), the most important of the four volumes of essays he published during the decade, and the one in which he first set himself unequivocally against what he regarded as the vulgarity and perversity of mass civilisation. Between September 1925 and June 1926 Huxley had travelled via India to the United States, and it was this visit to America which made him so pessimistic about the cultural future of Europe. He recounted his experiences in *Jesting Pilate* (1926). 'The thing which is happening in America is a revaluation of values,' Huxley wrote, 'a radical alteration (for the worse) of established standards', and it was soon after visiting the United States that Huxley conceived the idea of writing a satire on what he had encountered. *Brave New World* (1932) may be read as Huxley's contribution to the widespread fear of Americanisation which had been current in Europe since the mid-nineteenth century, but this humorous, disturbing and curiously ambivalent novel offers much more than straightforward travesty. Similarly, although *Brave New World* has become, with Orwell's *Nineteen Eighty-Four*, one of the twin pillars of the anti-utopian tradition in literature and a byword for all that is most repellent and 'nightmarish' in the world to come, it was written with Huxley's gaze very much on the crisis-torn present of Britain in 1931. When placed alongside *Brief Candles* (1930), a well-received collection of short stories, *Music at Night* (1931), a typically energetic and wide-ranging volume of essays, and *Texts and Pretexts* (1932), a verse anthology with commentaries designed to show that even in the highly-charged political atmosphere of the early 1930s 'they also serve who only bother their heads about art', Huxley's polygonal appeal as a novelist, thinker and pundit is brought home. In 1934 he published *Beyond the Mexique Bay*, an account of his travels in the Caribbean and Central America, and in 1936, *Eyeless in Gaza*. Stimulated by his conversion to pacifism in November 1935, Huxley's sixth novel imbricates the fears, foibles, prejudices and dissensions of the age with a fictionalisation of his own history. A commitment to questions which are essentially religious, rather than political or philosophical, is evident in Huxley's work for the first time.

When Huxley left Europe for the United States in April 1937 he was at the height of his fame as a novelist and the Peace Pledge Union's leading celebrity. Ironically, he was by now far more concerned with the virtues of non-attachment, anarchism, decentralisation and mystical salvation than with the failings of contemporary society, the role of pacifism in national politics or the art of fiction. If Huxley had been intent on exposing the meaninglessness of life in the 1920s, from the mid-1930s he was preoccupied with seeking the meaning of existence. *Ends and Means* (1937), in which Huxley tried 'to relate the problems of domestic and international politics, of war and economics, of education, religion and ethics, to a theory of the ultimate nature of reality', signalled his departure for the higher ground of mystical enlightenment where he would remain encamped for the rest of his life.

It was to lecture on the issues which dominate *Ends and Means* that Huxley and his friend and guru Gerald Heard had travelled to the United States. Huxley had every intention of returning to Europe, but his wife's need to live in a hot, dry climate on health grounds and the lucrative prospect of writing for the movies contrived to keep the Huxleys in America until it was too unsafe to return. Huxley's reaction to Hollywood and its cult of youth finds mordant expression in *After Many a Summer* (1939), the story of a Citizen Kane-like character's life of grandiose illusion. The materialist excesses of Jo Stoyte are counterpointed by the ascetic convictions of Propter, a modern-day anchorite modelled on Heard. Huxley and Hollywood were not compatible, and his failure to write a popular play in the inter-war years was mirrored in his largely unsuccessful efforts to write for the movies. Walt Disney's widely reported rejection of Huxley's synopsis of *Alice in Wonderland* on the grounds that he 'could only understand every third word' was symptomatic of Huxley's problem. His natural bent was for the leisurely and allusive development of an idea; above all else the movie moguls demanded pacey dialogue. His disenchantment with the world of the film studios is evident in the opening pages of *Ape and Essence* (1948), Huxley's ghastly and graphic projection of Los Angeles as a ruinous, sprawling ossuary in the aftermath of the atomic Third World War. While the threat of global nuclear conflict has receded for the present, Huxley's discussion of the rapid deforestation, pollution and other acts of ecological 'imbecility' which preceded the self-inflicted apocalypse he describes in the novel, is still chillingly topical.

Huxley spent most of the war years in a small house at Llano in the Mojave Desert in Southern California. In 1926 he had dismissed meditation as 'the doze's first cousin', but it was to a life of quietistic contemplation that Huxley now devoted himself. This phase of his career resulted in the excellent *Grey Eminence* (1941), a biography of Father Joseph, adviser to Cardinal Richelieu; *Time Must Have a Stop* (1944), a novel set in Florence in 1929 in which, to borrow Huxley's words, 'a piece of the *Comédie Humaine* . . . modulates into a version of the *Divina Commedia*'; and *The Perennial Philosophy* (1945), a profoundly influential anthology of excerpts and commentaries illustrating what Huxley called 'the highest common factor of all the higher religions'. He went on to say with typical humour and humility, 'The greatest merit of the book is that about forty per cent of it is not by me, but by a lot of saints, many of whom were also men of genius.' *The Devils of Loudun*, a compelling psychological study of sexual hysteria in seventeenth-century France, which was subsequently turned into a successful film, appeared in

1952. In the same way that Huxley's astringent social satires caught the mood of the 1920s, so, in the years during and following the Second World War and the enormity of the Jewish Holocaust, his personal concern with spiritual and ethical matters and his consternation at the accelerating arms race, reflected both the tone and unease of the zeitgeist.

Huxley also acquired new readers through his support of the marginal and unconventional, and his detractors, hitherto exercised by what they saw as his immorality or preachiness, began to pour scorn on his alleged faddism. In 1942 he published *The Art of Seeing*, a passionate defence of the Bates method of eye training which aroused a storm of protest from the optometrist lobby. Even more outrageous, for many, was his suggestion in *The Doors of Perception* (1954) and its sequel, *Heaven and Hell* (1956), that mescalin and lysergic acid were 'drugs of unique distinction' which should be exploited for the 'supernaturally brilliant' visionary experiences they offered to those with open minds and sound livers. *The Doors of Perception* is indeed a bewitching account of the inner shangri-la of the mescalin taker, where 'there is neither work nor monotony' but only 'a perpetual present made up of one continually changing apocalypse', where 'the divine source of all existence' is evident in a vase of flowers, and even the creases in a pair of trousers reveal 'a labyrinth of endlessly significant complexity'. Not surprisingly, *The Doors of Perception* became a set text for the beat generation and the psychedelic Sixties, The Doors naming their band after the book which also earned Huxley a place on the sleeve of The Beatles' *Sergeant Pepper* album.

Maria Huxley died in February 1955, shortly before Huxley published his penultimate novel, *The Genius and the Goddess*, in which John Rivers recounts the brief history of his disastrous involvement, when he was a 'virgin prig of twenty-eight', with the wife of his colleague Henry Maartens, a Nobel Prize-winning scientist. Not for the first time, Huxley's theme is the havoc which ensues when a man with an idealistic misconception of life born of a cloistered and emotionally deprived upbringing experiences the full, sensual impact of human passion.

Huxley married Laura Archera, a practising psychotherapist, in March 1956. Two years later he published *Brave New World Revisited*, in which he surveyed contemporary society in the light of his earlier predictions. Huxley's knack of keying in to the anxieties of the moment was as sharp as ever, and this touch is also evident in a series of lectures on 'The Human Situation' which he gave at Santa Barbara in 1959, published in one volume in 1977. Both books address problems which are no less pressing today, such as overpopulation, the recrudescence of nationalism and the fragility of the natural world. Huxley's last novel, *Island*, was published in 1962, the year in which he was made a Companion of Literature, and the year after his Los Angeles home and most of his personal effects had been destroyed in a fire which, Huxley said, left him 'a man without possessions and without a past'.

Island is the story of how the offshore utopia of Pala, where population growth has been stabilised and Mutual Adoption Clubs have superseded the tyranny of the family, and where *maithuna*, or the yoga of love and *moksha*, an hallucinogenic toadstool, ensure that the Palanese have little reason to feel disgruntled, falls victim to the age-old menaces of material progress and territorial expansionism. *Island* is perhaps Huxley's most pessimistic book, his poignant acknowledgement that in a world of increasing greed, mass communication, oil-guzzling transport, burgeoning population and inveterate hostility, a pacific and co-operative community like Pala's 'oasis of freedom and happiness' has little hope of survival. Soon after *Island* was published Huxley commented that the 'weakness of the book consists in a disbalance between fable and exposition. The story has too much weight, in the way of ideas and reflections, to carry.' But, while some readers would agree with this criticism, for others *Island* exemplifies Huxley's particular contribution to twentieth-century letters. In his early days the highbrow incarnate and a reluctant lecturer for the Peace Pledge Union, Huxley became for many a companionable polymath, a transatlantic sage at large, whose unending quest for synthesis and meaning in an ever-more perplexing and violent world provided a paradigm for their own search for peace and understanding.

Before his eyesight was damaged, Huxley's ambition was to specialise in the sciences, and it is significant that in his last published work, *Literature and Science* (1963), he pleads yet again for a *rapprochement* between the two cultures, arguing passionately against the contemporary stress on their dichotomy. The book begins by emphasising the wide-ranging erudition of T.H. Huxley and Matthew Arnold. Their descendant, one of the most stimulating and provocative writers of the twentieth century, proved himself a worthy inheritor of their abilities over the course of his long and varied career.

Huxley died of cancer at his home in Hollywood on 22 November 1963, unaware that President J.F. Kennedy had been assassinated earlier that afternoon in Dallas. In 1971 his ashes were returned to England and interred in his parents' grave at Compton in Surrey.

David Bradshaw
Worcester College, Oxford
1993

For M.

If the doors of perception were cleansed everything would appear to man as it is, infinite.

WILLIAM BLAKE

The Doors of Perception

It was in 1886 that the German pharmacologist, Ludwig Lewin, published the first systematic study of the cactus, to which his own name was subsequently given. *Anhalonium Lewinii* was new to science. To primitive religion and the Indians of Mexico and the American Southwest it was a friend of immemorially long standing. Indeed, it was much more than a friend. In the words of one of the early Spanish visitors to the New World, 'they eat a root which they call Peyotl, and which they venerate as though it were a deity.'

Why they should have venerated it as a deity became apparent when such eminent psychologists as Jaensch, Havelock Ellis and Weir Mitchell began their experiments with mescalin, the active principle of peyotl. True, they stopped short at a point well this side of idolatry; but all concurred in assigning to mescalin a position among drugs of unique distinction. Administered in suitable doses, it changes the quality of consciousness more profoundly and yet is less toxic than any other substance in the pharmacologist's repertory.

Mescalin research has been going on sporadically ever since the days of Lewin and Havelock Ellis. Chemists have not merely isolated the alkaloid; they have learned how to synthesize it, so that the supply no longer depends on the sparse and intermittent crop of a desert cactus. Alienists have dosed themselves with mescalin in the hope thereby of coming to a better, a first-hand understanding of their patients' mental processes. Working unfortunately upon too few subjects within

1

too narrow a range of circumstances, psychologists have observed and catalogued some of the drug's more striking effects. Neurologists and physiologists have found out something about the mechanism of its action upon the central nervous system. And at least one professional philosopher has taken mescalin for the light it may throw on such ancient unsolved riddles as the place of mind in nature and the relationship between brain and consciousness.

There matters rested until, two or three years ago, a new and perhaps highly significant fact was observed.[1] Actually the fact had been staring everyone in the face for several decades; but nobody, as it happened, had noticed it until a young English psychiatrist, at present working in Canada, was struck by the close similarity, in chemical composition, between mescalin and adrenalin. Further research revealed that lysergic acid, an extremely potent hallucinogen derived from ergot, has a structural biochemical relationship to the others. Then came the discovery that adrenochrome, which is a product of the decomposition of adrenalin, can produce many of the symptoms observed in mescalin intoxication. But adrenochrome probably occurs spontaneously in the human body. In other words, each

[1] See the following papers:

Schizophrenia: A New Approach. By Humphry Osmond and John Smythies. Journal of Mental Science. Vol. xcviii. April 1952.

On Being Mad. By Humphry Osmond. Saskatchewan Psychiatric Services Journal. Vol. i. No. 2. September 1952.

The Mescalin Phenomena. By John Smythies. The British Journal for the Philosophy of Science. Vol. iii. February 1953.

Schizophrenia: A New Approach. By Abram Hoffer, Humphry Osmond and John Smythies. The Journal of Mental Science. Vol. c. No. 418. January 1954.

Numerous other papers on the biochemistry, pharmacology, psychology and neurophysiology of schizophrenia and the mescalin phenomena are in preparation.

one of us may be capable of manufacturing a chemical, minute doses of which are known to cause profound changes in consciousness. Certain of these changes are similar to those which occur in that most characteristic plague of the twentieth century, schizophrenia. Is the mental disorder due to a chemical disorder? And is the chemical disorder due, in its turn, to psychological distresses affecting the adrenals? It would be rash and premature to affirm it. The most we can say is that some kind of a *prima facie* case has been made out. Meanwhile the clue is being systematically followed, the sleuths – biochemists, psychiatrists, psychologists – are on the trail.

By a series of, for me, extremely fortunate circumstances I found myself, in the spring of 1953, squarely athwart that trail. One of the sleuths had come on business to California. In spite of seventy years of mescalin research, the psychological material at his disposal was still absurdly inadequate, and he was anxious to add to it. I was on the spot and willing, indeed eager, to be a guinea-pig. Thus it came about that, one bright May morning, I swallowed four-tenths of a gramme of mescalin dissolved in half a glass of water and sat down to wait for the results.

We live together, we act on, and react to, one another; but always and in all circumstances we are by ourselves. The martyrs go hand in hand into the arena; they are crucified alone. Embraced, the lovers desperately try to fuse their insulated ecstasies into a single self-transcendence; in vain. By its very nature every embodied spirit is doomed to suffer and enjoy in solitude. Sensations, feelings, insights, fancies – all these are private and, except through symbols and at second hand, incommunicable. We can pool information about experiences,

3

but never the experiences themselves. From family to nation, every human group is a society of island universes.

Most island universes are sufficiently like one another to permit of inferential understanding or even of mutual empathy or 'feeling into.' Thus, remembering our own bereavements and humiliations, we can condole with others in analogous circumstances, can put ourselves (always, of course, in a slightly Pickwickian sense) in their places. But in certain cases communication between universes is incomplete or even non-existent. The mind is its own place, and the places inhabited by the insane and the exceptionally gifted are so different from the places where ordinary men and women live, that there is little or no common ground of memory to serve as a basis for understanding or fellow feeling. Words are uttered, but fail to enlighten. The things and events to which the symbols refer belong to mutually exclusive realms of experience.

To see ourselves as others see us is a most salutary gift. Hardly less important is the capacity to see others as they see themselves. But what if these others belong to a different species and inhabit a radically alien universe? For example, how can the sane get to know what it actually feels like to be mad? Or, short of being born again as a visionary, a medium or a musical genius, how can we ever visit the worlds which, to Blake, to Swedenborg, to Johann Sebastian Bach, were home? And how can a man at the extreme limits of ectomorphy and cerebrotonia ever put himself in the place of one at the limits of endomorphy and viscerotonia or, except within certain circumscribed areas, share the feelings of one who stands at the limits of mesomorphy and somatotonia? To the unmitigated behaviourist such questions, I suppose, are meaningless. But for those who theoretically believe what in practice they know to be true – namely, that there is an inside to experience as well as an outside – the problems posed are real problems, all the more grave for being, some completely insoluble, some soluble only in exceptional circumstances and by methods not available to every- one. Thus, it seems virtually certain that I shall never know what it feels like to be Sir John Falstaff or Joe Louis. On the other hand, it had always seemed to me possible that, through hypnosis, for example, or auto-hypnosis, by means of systematic meditation, or else by taking the appropriate drug, I might so change my ordinary mode of consciousness as to be able to know, from the inside, what the visionary, the medium, even the mystic were talking about.

From what I had read of the mescalin experience I was convinced in advance that the drug would admit me, at least for a few hours, into the kind of inner world described by Blake and Æ. But what I had expected did not happen. I had expected to lie with my eyes shut, looking at visions of many-coloured geometries, of animated architectures, rich with gems and fabulously lovely, of landscapes with heroic figures, of symbolic dramas trembling perpetually on the verge of the ultimate revelation. But I had not reckoned, it was evident, with the idiosyncrasies of my mental make-up, the facts of my temperament, training and habits.

I am and, for as long as I can remember, I have always been a poor visualizer. Words, even the pregnant words of poets, do not evoke pictures in my mind. No hypnagogic visions greet me on the verge of sleep. When I recall something, the memory does not present itself to me as a vividly seen event or object. By an effort of the will, I can evoke a not very vivid image of what happened yesterday afternoon, of how the Lungarno used to look before the bridges were destroyed, of the Bayswater Road when the only buses were green and tiny and drawn by aged horses at three and a half miles an hour. But such images have little substance and absolutely no autonomous life of their own. They stand to real, perceived objects in the same relation as Homer's ghosts stood to the men of flesh and blood, who came to visit them in the shades. Only when I have a high temperature do my mental images come to independent life. To those in whom the faculty of visualization is strong my inner world must seem curiously drab, limited and uninteresting. This was the world – a poor thing but my own – which I expected to see transformed into something completely unlike itself.

The change which actually took place in that world was in no sense revolutionary. Half an hour after swallowing the drug I became aware of a slow dance of golden lights. A little later there were sumptuous red surfaces swelling and expanding from bright nodes of energy that vibrated with a continuously changing, patterned life. At another time the closing of my eyes revealed a complex of grey structures, within which pale blueish spheres kept emerging into intense solidity and, having emerged, would slide noiselessly upwards, out of sight. But at no time were there faces or forms of men or animals. I saw no landscapes, no enormous spaces, no magical growth and metamorphosis of buildings, nothing remotely like a drama or a parable. The other world to which mescalin admitted me was not the world of visions; it existed out there, in what I could see with my eyes open. The great change was in the realm of objective fact. What had happened to my subjective universe was relatively unimportant.

I took my pill at eleven. An hour and half later I was sitting in my study, looking intently at a small glass vase. The vase contained only three flowers – a full-blown Belle of Portugal rose, shell pink with a hint at every petal's base of a hotter, flamier hue; a large magenta and cream-coloured carnation; and, pale purple at the end of its broken stalk, the bold heraldic blossom of an iris. Fortuitous and provisional, the little nosegay broke all the rules of traditional good taste. At breakfast that morning I had been struck by the lively dissonance of its colours. But that was no longer the point. I was not looking now at an unusual flower arrangement. I was seeing what Adam had seen on the morning of his creation – the miracle, moment by moment, of naked existence.

'Is it agreeable?' somebody asked. (During this part of the experiment, all conversations were recorded on a dictating machine, and it has been possible for me to refresh my memory of what was said.)

'Neither agreeable nor disagreeable,' I answered. 'It just *is*.'

Istigkeit – wasn't that the word Meister Eckhart liked to use? 'Is-ness.' The Being of Platonic philosophy – except that Plato seems to have made the enormous, the grotesque mistake of separating Being from becoming, and identifying it with the mathematical abstraction of the Idea. He could never, poor fellow, have seen a bunch of flowers shining with their own inner light and all but quivering under the pressure of the significance with which they were charged; could never have perceived that what rose and iris and carnation so intensely signified was nothing more, and nothing less, than what they were – a transience that was yet eternal life, a

7

perpetual perishing that was at the same time pure Being, a bundle of minute, unique particulars in which, by some unspeakable and yet self-evident paradox, was to be seen the divine source of all existence.

I continued to look at the flowers, and in their living light I seemed to detect the qualitative equivalent of breathing – but of a breathing without returns to a starting-point, with no recurrent ebbs but only a repeated flow from beauty to heightened beauty, from deeper to ever deeper meaning. Words like Grace and Transfiguration came to my mind, and this of course was what, among other things, they stood for. My eyes travelled from the rose to the carnation, and from that feathery incandescence to the smooth scrolls of sentient amethyst which were the iris. The Beatific Vision, *Sat Chit Ananda*, Being-Awareness-Bliss – for the first time I understood, not on the verbal level, not by inchoate hints or at a distance, but precisely and completely what those prodigious syllables referred to. And then I remembered a passage I had read in one of Suzuki's essays. 'What is the Dharma-Body of the Buddha?' (The Dharma-Body of the Buddha is another way of saying Mind, Suchness, the Void, the Godhead.) The question is asked in a Zen monastery by an earnest and bewildered novice. And with the prompt irrelevance of one of the Marx Brothers, the Master answers, 'The hedge at the bottom of the garden.' 'And the man who realizes this truth,' the novice dubiously enquires, 'what, may I ask, is he?' Groucho gives him a whack over the shoulders with his staff and answers, 'A golden-haired lion.'

It had been, when I read it, only a vaguely pregnant piece of nonsense. Now it was all as clear as day, as evident as Euclid. Of course the Dharma-Body of the Buddha was the hedge at the bottom of the garden. At

8

the same time, and no less obviously, it was these flowers, it was anything that I – or rather the blessed Not-I released for a moment from my throttling embrace – cared to look at. The books, for example, with which my study walls were lined. Like the flowers, they glowed, when I looked at them, with brighter colours, a profounder significance. Red books, like rubies; emerald books; books bound in white jade; books of agate, of aquamarine, of yellow topaz; lapis lazuli books whose colour was so intense, so intrinsically meaningful, that they seemed to be on the point of leaving the shelves to thrust themselves more insistently on my attention.

'What about spatial relationships?' the investigator enquired, as I was looking at the books.

It was difficult to answer. True, the perspective looked rather odd, and the walls of the room no longer seemed to meet in right angles. But these were not the really important facts. The really important facts were that spatial relationships had ceased to matter very much and that my mind was perceiving the world in terms of other than spatial categories. At ordinary times the eye concerns itself with such problems as *Where? – How far? – How situated in relation to what?* In the mescalin experience the implied questions to which the eye responds are of another order. Place and distance cease to be of much interest. The mind does its perceiving in terms of intensity of existence, profundity of significance, relationships within a pattern. I saw the books, but was not at all concerned with their positions in space. What I noticed, what impressed itself upon my mind was the fact that all of them glowed with living light and that in some the glory was more manifest than in others. In this context, position and the three dimensions were beside the point. Not, of course, that the category of space had been abolished. When I got up and walked about, I could do so quite normally, without misjudging the whereabouts of objects. Space was still there; but it had lost its predominance. The mind was primarily concerned, not with measures and locations, but with being and meaning.

And along with indifference to space there went an even completer indifference to time.

'There seems to be plenty of it,' was all I would answer when the investigator asked me to say what I felt about time.

Plenty of it, but exactly how much was entirely irrelevant. I could, of course, have looked at my watch; but my watch, I knew, was in another universe. My actual experience had been, was still, of an indefinite duration or alternatively of a perpetual present made up of one continually changing apocalypse.

From the books the investigator directed my attention to the furniture. A small typing-table stood in the centre of the room; beyond it, from my point of view, was a wicker chair and beyond that a desk. The three pieces formed an intricate pattern of horizontals, uprights and diagonals – a pattern all the more interesting for not being interpreted in terms of spatial relationships. Table, chair and desk came together in a composition that was like something by Braque or Juan Gris, a still life recognizably related to the objective world, but rendered without depth, without any attempt at photographic realism. I was looking at my furniture, not as the utilitarian who has to sit on chairs, to write at desks and tables, and not as the camera-man or scientific recorder, but as the pure aesthete whose concern is only with forms and their relationships within the field of vision or the picture space. But as I looked, this purely aesthetic Cubist's-eye view gave place to what I can only describe as the sacramental vision of reality. I was back where I had been when I was looking at the flowers – back in a world where everything shone with the Inner Light, and was infinite in its significance. The legs, for example of that chair – how miraculous their tubularity, how supernatural their polished smoothness! I spent several minutes – or was it several centuries? – not merely gazing at those bamboo legs, but actually *being* them – or rather being myself in them; or, to be still more accurate (for 'I' was not involved in the case, nor in a certain sense were 'they') being my Not-self in the Not-self which was the chair.

Reflecting on my experience, I find myself agreeing with the eminent Cambridge philosopher, Dr C. D. Broad, 'that we should do well to consider much more seriously than we have hitherto been inclined to do the type of theory which Bergson put forward in connection with memory and sense perception. The suggestion is that the function of the brain and nervous system and sense organs is in the main *eliminative* and not productive. Each person is at each moment capable of remembering all that has ever happened to him and of perceiving everything that is happening everywhere in the universe. The function of the brain and nervous system is to protect us from being overwhelmed and confused by this mass of largely useless and irrelevant knowledge, by shutting out most of what we should otherwise perceive or remember at any moment, and leaving only that very small and special selection which is likely to be practically useful.' According to such a theory, each one of us is potentially Mind at Large. But in so far as we are animals, our business is at all costs to survive. To make biological survival possible, Mind at Large has to be funnelled through the reducing valve of the brain and nervous system. What comes out at the other end is a measly trickle of the kind of consciousness which will help us to stay alive on the surface of this particular planet. To formulate and express the contents of this reduced awareness, man has invented and endlessly elaborated those symbol-systems and implicit philosophies which we call languages. Every individual is at once the beneficiary and the victim of the linguistic tradition into which he or she has been born – the beneficiary inasmuch as language gives access to the accumulated records of other people's experience, the victim in so far as it confirms him in the belief that reduced awareness is the only awareness and as it bedevils his sense of reality, so that he is all too apt to take his concepts for data, his words for actual things. That which, in the language of religion, is called 'this world' is the universe of reduced awareness, expressed and, as it were, petrified by language. The various 'other worlds,' with which human beings erratically make contact are so many elements in the totality of the awareness belonging to Mind at Large. Most people, most of the time, know only what comes through the reducing valve and is consecrated as genuinely real by the local language. Certain persons, however, seem to be born with a kind of by-pass that circumvents the reducing valve. In others temporary by-passes may be acquired either spontaneously, or as the result of deliberate 'spiritual exercises,' or through hypnosis, or by means of drugs. Through these permanent or temporary by-passes there flows, not indeed the perception 'of everything that is happening everywhere in the universe' (for the by-pass does not abolish the reducing valve, which still excludes the total content of Mind at Large), but something more than, and above all something different from, the carefully selected utilitarian material which our narrowed, individual minds regard as a complete, or at least sufficient, picture of reality.

The brain is provided with a number of enzyme systems which serve to co-ordinate its workings. Some of these enzymes regulate the supply of glucose to the brain cells. Mescalin inhibits the production of these enzymes and thus lowers the amount of glucose available to an organ that is in constant need of sugar. When mescalin reduces the brain's normal ration of sugar, what happens? Too few cases have been observed, and therefore a comprehensive answer cannot yet be given. But what happens to the majority of the few who have taken mescalin under supervision can be summarized as follows.

(1) The ability to remember and to 'think straight' is little if at all reduced. (Listening to the recordings of my conversation under the influence of the drug, I cannot discover that I was then any stupider than I am at ordinary times.)

(2) Visual impressions are greatly intensified and the eye recovers some of the perceptual innocence of childhood, when the sensum was not immediately and automatically subordinated to the concept. Interest in space is diminished and interest in time falls almost to zero.

(3) Though the intellect remains unimpaired and though perception is enormously improved, the will suffers a profound change for the worse. The mescalin taker sees no reason for doing anything in particular and finds most of the causes for which, at ordinary times, he

was prepared to act and suffer, profoundly uninteresting. He can't be bothered with them, for the good reason that he has better things to think about.

(4) These better things may be experienced (as I experienced them) 'out there,' or 'in here,' or in both worlds, the inner and the outer, simultaneously or successively. That they *are* better seems to be self-evident to all mescalin takers who come to the drug with a sound liver and an untroubled mind.

These effects of mescalin are the sort of effects you could expect to follow the administration of a drug having the power to impair the efficiency of the cerebral reducing valve. When the brain runs out of sugar, the undernourished ego grows weak, can't be bothered to undertake the necessary chores, and loses all interest in those spatial and temporal relationships which mean so much to an organism bent on getting on in the world. As Mind at Large seeps past the no longer watertight valve, all kinds of biologically useless things start to happen. In some cases there may be extra-sensory perceptions. Other persons discover a world of visionary beauty. To others again is revealed the glory, the infinite value and meaningfulness of naked existence, of the given, unconceptualized event. In the final stage of egolessness there is an 'obscure knowledge' that All is in all – that All is actually each. This is as near, I take it, as a finite mind can ever come to 'perceiving everything that is happening everywhere in the universe.'

In this context, how significant is the enormous heightening, under mescalin, of the perception of colour! For certain animals it is biologically very important to be able to distinguish certain hues. But beyond the limits of their utilitarian spectrum, most creatures are completely colour blind. Bees, for example, spend most of their time 'deflowering the fresh virgins of the spring'; but, as von Frisch has shown, they can recognize only a very few colours. Man's highly developed colour sense is a biological luxury – inestimably precious to him as an intellectual and spiritual being, but unnecessary to his survival as an animal. To judge by the adjectives which Homer puts into their mouths, the heroes of the Trojan War hardly excelled the bees in their capacity to distinguish colours. In this respect, at least, mankind's advance has been prodigious.

Mescalin raises all colours to a higher power and makes the percipient aware of innumerable fine shades of difference, to which, at ordinary times, he is completely blind. It would seem that, for Mind at Large, the so-called secondary characters of things are primary. Unlike Locke, it evidently feels that colours are more important, better worth attending to than masses, positions and dimensions. Like mescalin takers, many mystics perceive supernaturally brilliant colours, not only with the inward eye, but even in the objective world around them. Similar reports are made by psychics and sensitives. There are certain mediums to whom the mescalin taker's brief revelation is a matter, during long periods, of daily and hourly experience.

From this long but indispensable excursion into the realm of theory we may now return to the miraculous facts – four bamboo chair legs in the middle of a room. Like Wordsworth's daffodils, they brought all manner of wealth – the gift, beyond price, of a new direct insight into the very Nature of Things, together with a more modest treasure of understanding in the field, especially, of the arts.

A rose is a rose is a rose. But these chair legs were

chair legs were St Michael and all angels. Four or five hours after the event, when the effects of a cerebral sugar shortage were wearing off, I was taken for a little tour of the city, which included a visit, towards sundown, to what is modestly claimed to be The World's Biggest Drug Store. At the Back of the W.B.D.S., among the toys, the greeting cards and comics stood a row, surprisingly enough, of art books. I picked up the first volume that came to hand. It was on Van Gogh, and the picture at which the book opened was *The Chair* – that astounding portrait of a *Ding an Sich*, which the mad painter saw, with a kind of adoring terror, and tried to render on his canvas. But it was a task to which the power even of genius proved wholly inadequate. The chair Van Gogh had seen was obviously the same in essence as the chair I had seen. But, though incomparably more real than the chair of ordinary perception, the chair in his picture remained no more than an unusually expressive symbol of the fact. The fact had been manifested Suchness; this was only an emblem. Such emblems are sources of true knowledge about the Nature of Things, and this true knowledge may serve to prepare the mind which accepts it for immediate insights on its own account. But that is all. However expressive, symbols can never be the things they stand for.

It would be interesting, in this context, to make a study of the works of art available to the great knowers of Suchness. What sort of pictures did Eckhart look at? What sculptures and paintings played a part in the religious experience of St John of the Cross, of Hakuin, of Hui-neng, of William Law? The questions are beyond my power to answer; but I strongly suspect that most of the great knowers of Suchness paid very little attention to art – some refusing to have anything to do with it at all, others being content with what a critical eye would regard as second-rate, or even tenth-rate, works. (To a person whose transfigured and transfiguring mind can see the All in every *this*, the first-rateness or tenth-rateness of even a religious painting will be a matter of the most sovereign indifference.) Art, I suppose, is only for beginners, or else for those resolute dead-enders, who have made up their minds to be content with the *ersatz* of Suchness, with symbols rather than with what they signify, with the elegantly composed recipe in lieu of actual dinner.

I returned the Van Gogh to its rack and picked up the volume standing next to it. It was a book on Botticelli. I turned the pages. *The Birth of Venus* – never one of my favourites. *Venus and Mars*, that loveliness so passionately denounced by poor Ruskin at the height of his long-drawn-out sexual tragedy. The marvellously rich and intricate *Calumny of Apelles*. And then a somewhat less familiar and not very good picture, *Judith*. My attention was arrested and I gazed in fascination, not at the pale neurotic heroine or her attendant, not at the victim's hairy head or the vernal landscape in the background, but at the purplish silk of Judith's pleated bodice and long wind-blown skirts.

This was something I had seen before – seen that very morning, between the flowers and the furniture, when I looked down by chance, and went on passionately staring by choice, at my own crossed legs. Those folds in the trousers – what a labyrinth of endlessly significant complexity! And the texture of the grey flannel – how rich, how deeply, mysteriously sumptuous! And here they were again, in Botticelli's picture.

Civilized human beings wear clothes, therefore there can be no portraiture, no mythological or historical story telling without representations of folded textiles. But though it may account for the origins, mere tailoring can never explain the luxuriant development of drapery as a major theme of all the plastic arts. Artists, it is obvious, have always loved drapery for its own sake – or, rather, for their own. When you paint or carve drapery, you are painting or carving forms which, for all practical purposes, are non-representational – the kind of unconditioned forms on which artists even in the most naturalistic tradition like to let themselves go. In the average Madonna or Apostle the strictly human, fully representational element accounts for about ten per cent. of the whole. All the rest consists of many coloured variations on the inexhaustible theme of crumpled wool or linen. And these non-representational nine-tenths of a Madonna or an Apostle may be just as important qualitatively as they are in quantity. Very often they set the tone of the whole work of art, they state the key in which the theme is being rendered, they express the mood, the temperament, the attitude to life of the artist. Stoical serenity reveals itself in the smooth surfaces, the broad untortured folds of Piero's draperies. Torn between fact and wish, between cynicism and idealism, Bernini tempers the all but caricatural verisimilitude of his faces with enormous sartorial abstractions, which are the embodiment, in stone or bronze, of the everlasting commonplaces of rhetoric – the heroism, the holiness, the sublimity to which mankind perpetually aspires, for the most part in vain. And here are El Greco's disquietingly visceral skirts and mantles; here are the sharp, twisting, flame-like folds in which Cosimo Tura clothes his figures: in the first, traditional spirituality breaks down into a nameless physiological yearning; in the second, there writhes an agonized sense of the world's essential strangeness and hostility. Or consider Watteau; his men and women play lutes, get ready for balls and harlequinades, embark, on velvet lawns an under noble trees, for the Cythera of every lover's dream; their enormous melancholy and the flayed, excruciating sensibility of their creator find expression, not in the actions recorded, not in the gestures and the faces portrayed, but in the relief and texture of their taffeta skirts, their satin capes and doublets. Not an inch of smooth surface here, not a moment of peace or confidence, only a silken wilderness of countless tiny pleats and wrinkles, with an incessant modulation – inner uncertainty rendered with the perfect assurance of a master hand – of tone into tone, of one indeterminate colour into another. In life, man proposes, God disposes. In the plastic arts the proposing is done by the subject matter; that which disposes is ultimately the artist's temperament, proximately (at least in portraiture, history and genre) the carved or painted drapery. Between them these two may decree that a *fête galante* shall move to tears, that a crucifixion shall be serene to the point of cheerfulness, that a stigmatization shall be almost intolerably sexy, that the likeness of a prodigy of female brainlessness (I am thinking now of Ingres' incomparable Mme Moitessier) shall express the austerest, the most uncompromising intellectuality.

But this is not the whole story. Draperies, as I had now discovered, are much more than devices for the introduction of non-representational forms into naturalistic paintings and sculptures. What the rest of us see only under the influence of mescalin, the artist is congenitally equipped to see all the time. His perception is not limited to what is biologically or socially useful. A little of the knowledge belonging to Mind at Large oozes past the reducing value of brain and ego into his consciousness. It is a knowledge of the intrinsic significance of every existent. For the artist as for the mescalin taker, draperies are living hieroglyphs that stand in some peculiarly expressive way for the unfathomable mystery of pure being. More even than the chair, though less perhaps than those wholly supernatural flowers, the folds of my grey flannel trousers were charged with 'is-ness.' To what they owed this privileged status, I cannot say. Is it, perhaps, because the forms of folded drapery are so strange and dramatic that they catch the eye and in this way force the miraculous fact of sheer existence upon the attention? Who knows? What is important is less the reason for the experience than the experience itself. Poring over Judith's skirts, there in the World's Biggest Drug Store, I knew that Botticelli – and not Botticelli alone, but many others too – had looked at draperies with the same transfigured and transfiguring eyes as had been mine that morning. They had seen the *Istigkeit*, the Allness and Infinity of folded cloth and had done their best to render it in paint or stone. Necessarily, of course, without success. For the glory and the wonder of pure existence belong to another order, beyond the power of even the highest art to express. But in Judith's skirt I could clearly see what, if I had been a painter of genius, I might have made of my old grey flannels. Not much, heaven knows, in comparison with the reality; but enough to delight generation after generation of beholders, enough to make them understand at least a little of the true significance of what, in our pathetic imbecility, we call 'mere things' and disregard in favour of television.

'This is how one ought to see,' I kept saying as I looked down at my trousers, or glanced at the jewelled books in the shelves, at the legs of my infinitely more than Van-Goghian chair. 'This is how one ought to see, how things really are.' And yet there were reservations. For if one always saw like this, one would never want to do anything else. Just looking, just being the divine Not-self of flower, of book, of chair, of flannel. That would be enough. But in that case what about other people? What about human relations? In the recording of that morning's conversations I find the question constantly repeated 'What about human relations?' How could one reconcile this timeless bliss of seeing as one ought to see with the temporal duties of doing what one ought to do and feeling as one ought to feel? 'One ought to be able,' I said, 'to see these trousers as infinitely important and human beings as still more infinitely important.' One ought – but in practice it seemed to be impossible. This participation in the manifest glory of things left no room, so to speak, for the ordinary, the necessary concerns of human existence, above all for concerns involving persons. For persons are selves and, in one respect at least, I was now a Not-self, simultaneously perceiving and being the Not-self of the things around me. To this new-born Not-self, the behaviour, the appearance, the very thought of the self it had momentarily ceased to be, and of other selves, its one-time fellows, seemed not indeed distasteful (for distastefulness was not one of the categories in terms of which I was thinking), but enormously irrelevant. Compelled by the investigator to analyse and report on what I was doing (and how I longed to be left alone with Eternity in a flower, Infinity in four chair legs and the Absolute in the folds of a pair of flannel trousers!) I realized that I was deliberately avoiding the eyes of those who were with me in the room, deliberately refraining from being too much aware of them. One was my wife, the other a man I respected and greatly liked; but both belonged to the world from which, for the moment, mescalin had delivered me – the world of selves, of time, of moral judgments and utilitarian considerations, the world (and it was this aspect of human life which I wished, above all else, to forget) of self-assertion, of cocksureness, of over-valued words and idolatrously worshipped notions.

At this stage of the proceedings I was handed a large coloured reproduction of the well-known self-portrait by Cézanne – the head and shoulders of a man in a large straw hat, red-cheeked, red-lipped, with rich black whiskers and a dark unfriendly eye. It is a magnificent painting; but it was not as a painting that I now saw it. For the head promptly took on a third dimension and came to life as a small goblin-like man looking out through a window in the page before me. I started to laugh. And when they asked me why, 'What pretensions!' I kept repeating. 'Who on earth does he think he is?' The question was not addressed to Cézanne in particular, but to the human species at large. Who did they all think they were?

'It's like Arnold Bennett in the Dolomites,' I said, suddenly remembering a scene, happily immortalized in a snapshot of A. B. some four or five years before his death toddling along a wintry road at Cortina d'Ampezzo. Around him lay the virgin snow; in the background was a more than gothic aspiration of red crags. And there was dear, kind, unhappy A. B. consciously overacting the role of his favourite character in fiction, himself, the Card in person. There he went, toddling slowly in the bright Alpine sunshine, his thumbs in the arm-holes of a yellow waistcoat which bulged, a little lower down, with the graceful curve of a Regency bow window at Brighton – his head thrown back as though to aim some stammered utterance, howitzer-like, at the blue dome of heaven. What he actually said, I have forgotten; but what his whole manner, air and posture fairly shouted was, 'I'm as good as those damned mountains.' And in some ways, of course, he was infinitely better; but not, as he knew very well, in the way his favourite character in fiction liked to imagine.

Successfully (whatever that may mean) or unsuccessfully, we all overact the part of our favourite character in fiction. And the fact, the almost infinitely unlikely fact, of actually being Cézanne makes no difference. For the consummate painter, with his little pipe-line to Mind at Large by-passing the brain-valve and ego-filter, was also and just as genuinely this whiskered goblin with the unfriendly eye.

For relief I turned back to the folds in my trousers. 'This is how one ought to see,' I repeated yet again. And I might have added, 'These are the sort of things one ought to look at.' Things without pretensions, satisfied to be merely themselves, sufficient in their suchness, not acting a part, not trying, insanely, to go it alone, in isolation from the Dharma-Body, in Luciferian defiance of the grace of God.

'The nearest approach to this,' I said, 'would be a Vermeer.'

Yes, a Vermeer. For that mysterious artist was trebly gifted – with the vision that perceives the Dharma-Body as the hedge at the bottom of the garden, with the talent to render as much of the vision as the limitations of human capacity permit, and with the prudence to confine himself in his paintings to the more manageable aspects of reality; for though Vermeer represented human beings, he was always a painter of still life. Cézanne, who told his female sitters to do their best to look like apples, tried to paint portraits in the same spirit. But his pippin-like women are more nearly related to Plato's Ideas than to the Dharma-Body in the hedge. They are Eternity and Infinity seen, not in sand or flower, but in the abstractions of some very superior band of geometry, Vermeer never asked his girls to look like apples. On the contrary, he insisted on their being girls to the very limit – but always with the proviso that they refrain from behaving girlishly. They might sit or quietly stand but never giggle, never display self-consciousness, never say their prayers or pine for absent sweethearts, never gossip, never gaze enviously at other women's babies, never flirt, never love nor hate nor work. In the act of doing any of these things they would doubtless become more intensely themselves, but would cease, for that very reason, to manifest their divine essential Not-self. In Blake's phrase, the doors of Vermeer's perception were only partially cleansed. A single panel had become almost perfectly transparent; the rest of the door was still muddy. The essential Not-self could be perceived very clearly in things and in living creatures on the hither side of good and evil. In human beings it was visible only when they were in repose, their minds untroubled, their bodies motionless. In these circumstances Vermeer could see Suchness in all its heavenly beauty – could see and, in some small measure, render it in a subtle and sumptuous still life. Vermeer is undoubtedly the greatest painter of human still lives. But there have been others, for example, Vermeer's French contemporaries, the Le Nain brothers. They set out, I suppose, to be *genre* painters; but what they actually produced was a series of human still lives, in which their cleansed perception of the infinite significance of all things is rendered not, as with Vermeer, by a subtle enrichment of colour, and texture, but by a heightened clarity, an obsessive distinctness of form, within an austere, almost monochromatic tonality. In our own day we have had Vuillard, the painter, at his best, of unforgettably splendid pictures of the Dharma-Body manifested in a bourgeois bedroom, of the Absolute blazing away in the midst of some stockbroker's family in a suburban garden, taking tea.

> *Ce qui fait que l'ancien bandagiste renie*
> *Le comptoir dont le faste alléchait les passants,*
> *C'est son jardin d'Auteuil, où, veufs de tout encens,*
> *Les Zinnias ont l'air d'être en tôle vernie.*

For Laurent Taillade the spectacle was merely obscene. But if the retired rubber goods merchant had sat still enough, Vuillard would have seen in him only the Dharma-Body, would have painted, in the zinnias, the goldfish pool, the villa's Moorish tower and Chinese lanterns, a corner of Eden before the Fall.

But meanwhile my question remained unanswered. How was this cleansed perception to be reconciled with a proper concern with human relations, with the necessary chores and duties, to say nothing of charity and practical compassion? The age-old debate between the actives and the contemplatives was being renewed – renewed, so far as I was concerned, with an unprecedented poignancy. For until this morning I had known contemplation only in its humbler, its more ordinary forms – as discursive thinking; as a rapt absorption in poetry or painting or music; as a patient waiting upon those inspirations, without which even the prosiest writer cannot hope to accomplish anything; as occasional glimpses, in nature, of Wordsworth's 'something far more deeply interfused'; as systematic silence leading, sometimes, to hints of an 'obscure knowledge.' But now I knew contemplation at its height. At its height, but not yet in its fullness. For in its fullness the way of Mary includes the way of Martha and raises it, so to speak, to its own higher power. Mescalin opens up the way of Mary, but shuts the door on that of Martha. It gives access to contemplation – but to a contemplation that is incompatible with action and even with the will to action, the very thought of action. In the intervals between his revelations the mescalin taker is apt to feel that, though in one way everything is supremely as it should be, in another there is something wrong. His problem is essentially the same as that which confronts the quietist, the *arhat* and, on another level, the landscape painter and the painter of human still lives. Mescalin can never solve that problem: it can only pose it, apocalyptically, for those to whom it had never before presented itself. The full and final solution can be found only by those who are prepared to implement the right kind of *Weltanschauung* by means of the right kind of behaviour and the right kind of constant and unstrained alertness. Over against the quietist stands the active-contemplative, the saint, the man who, in Eckhart's phrase, is ready to come down from the seventh heaven in order to bring a cup of water to his sick brother. Over against the *arhat*, retreating from appearances into an entirely transcendental Nirvana, stands the Bodhisattva, for whom Suchness and the world of contingencies are one, and for whose bound-less compassion every one of those contingencies is an occasion not only for transfiguring insight, but also for the most practical charity. And in the universe of art, over against Vermeer and the other painters of human still lives, over against the masters of Chinese and Japanese landscape painting, over against Constable and Turner, against Sisley and Seurat and Cézanne stands the all-inclusive art of Rembrandt. These are enormous names, inaccessible eminences. For myself, on this memorable May morning, I could only be grateful for an experience which had shown me, more clearly than I have ever seen it before, the true nature of the challenge and the completely liberating response.

Let me add, before we leave this subject, that there is no form of contemplation, even the most quietistic, which is without its ethical values. Half at least of all morality is negative and consists in keeping out of mischief. The Lord's prayer is less than fifty words long, and six of those words are devoted to asking God not to lead us into temptation. The one-sided contemplative leaves undone many things that he ought to do; but to make up for it he refrains from doing a host of things he ought not to do. The sum of evil, Pascal remarked, would be much diminished if men could only learn to sit quietly in their rooms. The contemplative whose perception has been cleansed does not have to stay in his room. He can go about his business, so completely satisfied to see and be a part of the divine Order of Things that he will never even be tempted to indulge in what Traherne called 'the dirty Devices of the world.' When we feel ourselves to be sole heirs of the universe, when 'the sea flows in our veins ... and the stars are our jewels,' when all things are perceived as infinite and holy, what motive can we have for covetousness or self-assertion, for the pursuit of power or the drearier forms of pleasure? Contemplatives are not likely to become gamblers, or procurers, or drunkards; they do not as a rule preach intolerance, or make war; do not find it necessary to rob, swindle or grind the faces of the poor. And to these enormous negative virtues we may add another which, though hard to define, is both positive and important. The *arhat* and the quietist may not practise contemplation in its fullness; but if they practise it at all, they may bring back enlightening reports of another, a transcendent country of the mind; and if they practise it in the height, they will become conduits through which some beneficent influence can flow out of that other country into a world of darkened selves, chronically dying for lack of it.

Meanwhile I had turned, at the investigator's request, from the portrait of Cézanne to what was going on, inside my head, when I shut my eyes. This time, the inscape was curiously unrewarding. The field of vision was filled with brightly coloured, constantly changing structures that seemed to be made of plastic or enamelled tin.

'Cheap,' I commented. 'Trivial. Like things in a Five and Ten.'

And all this shoddiness existed in a closed, cramped universe.

'It's as though one were below decks in a ship,' I said. 'A five-and-ten-cent ship.'

And as I looked, it became very clear that this five-and-ten-cent ship was in some way connected with human pretensions. This suffocating interior of a dime-store ship was my own personal self; these gimcrack mobiles of tin and plastic were my personal contributions to the universe.

I felt the lesson to be salutary, but was sorry, none the less, that it had had to be administered at this moment and in this form. As a rule the mescalin taker discovers an inner world as manifestly a datum, as self-evidently infinite and holy, as that transfigured outer world which I had seen with my eyes open. From the first, my own case had been different. Mescalin had endowed me temporarily with the power to see things with my eyes shut; but it could not, or at least on this occasion did not, reveal an inscape remotely comparable to my flowers or chair or flannels 'out there.' What it had allowed me to perceive, inside, was not the Dharma-Body in images, but my own mind; not archetypal Suchness, but a set of symbols – in other words, a home-made substitute for Suchness.

Most visualizers are transformed by mescalin into visionaries. Some of them – and they are perhaps more numerous than is generally supposed – require no transformation; they are visionaries all the time. The mental species to which Blake belonged is fairly widely distributed even in the urban-industrial societies of the present day. The poet-artist's uniqueness does not consist in the fact that (to quote from his *Descriptive Catalogue*) he actually *saw* 'those wonderful originals called in the Sacred Scriptures the Cherubim.' It does not consist in the fact that 'these wonderful originals seen in my visions were some of them one hundred feet in height ... all containing mythological and recondite meaning.' It consists solely in his ability to render, in words or (somewhat less successfully) in line and colour, some hint at least of a not excessively uncommon experience. The untalented visionary may perceive an

29

inner reality no less tremendous, beautiful and significant than the world beheld by Blake; but he lacks altogether the ability to express, in literary or plastic symbols, what he has seen.

From the records of religion and the surviving monuments of poetry and the plastic arts it is very plain that, at most times and in most places, men have attached more importance to the inscape than to objective existents, have felt that what they saw with their eyes shut possessed a spiritually higher significance than what they saw with their eyes open. The reason? Familiarity breeds contempt, and how to survive is a problem ranging in urgency from the chronically tedious to the excruciating. The outer world is what we wake up to every morning of our lives, is the place where, willy-nilly, we must try to make our living. In the inner world there is neither work nor monotony. We visit it only in dreams and musings, and its strangeness is such that we never find the same world on two successive occasions. What wonder, then, if human beings in their search for the divine have generally preferred to look within! Generally, but not always. In their art no less than in their religion, the Taoists and the Zen Buddhists looked beyond visions to the Void, and through the Void at 'the ten thousand things' of objective reality. Because of their doctrine of the Word made flesh, Christians should have been able, from the first, to adopt a similar attitude towards the universe around them. But because of the doctrine of the Fall, they found it very hard to do so. As recently as three hundred years ago an expression of thorough-going world denial and even world condemnation was both orthodox and comprehensible. 'We should feel wonder at nothing at all in Nature, except only the Incarnation of Christ.' In the seventeenth century, Lallemant's phrase seemed to make sense. To-day it has the ring of madness.

In China the rise of landscape painting to the rank of a major art form took place about a thousand, in Japan about six hundred and in Europe about three hundred years ago. The equation of Dharma-Body with hedge was made by those Zen Masters, who wedded Taoist naturalism with Buddhist transcendentalism. It was, therefore, only in the Far East that landscape painters consciously regarded their art as religious. In the West religious painting was a matter of portraying sacred personages, of illustrating hallowed texts. Landscape painters regarded themselves as secularists. To-day we recognize in Seurat one of the supreme masters of what may be called mystical landscape painting. And yet this man who was able, more effectively than any other, to render the One in the many, became quite indignant when somebody praised him for the 'poetry' of his work. 'I merely apply the System,' he protested. In other words he was merely a *pointilliste* and, in his own eyes, nothing else. A similar anecdote is told of John Constable. One day towards the end of his life, Blake met Constable at Hampstead and was shown one of the younger artist's sketches. In spite of his contempt for naturalistic art, the old visionary knew a good thing when he saw it – except, of course, when it was by Rubens. 'This is not drawing,' he cried, 'this is inspiration!' 'I had meant it to be drawing,' was Constable's characteristic answer. Both men were right. It *was* drawing, precise and veracious, and at the same time it *was* inspiration – inspiration of an order at least as high as Blake's. The pine trees on the Heath had actually been seen as identical with the Dharma-Body.

The sketch was a rendering, necessarily imperfect but still profoundly impressive, of what a cleansed perception had revealed to the open eyes of a great painter. From a contemplation, in the tradition of Wordsworth and Whitman, of the Dharma-Body as hedge, and from visions, such as Blake's, of the 'wonderful originals' within the mind, contemporary poets have retreated into an investigation of the personal, as opposed to the more than personal, subconscious and to a rendering, in highly abstract terms, not of the given, objective fact, but of mere scientific and theological notions. And something similar has happened in the field of painting. Here we have witnessed a general retreat from landscape, the predominant art form of the nineteenth century. This retreat from landscape has not been into that other, inner divine Datum, with which most of the traditional schools of the past were concerned, that Archetypal World, where men have always found the raw materials of myth and religion. No, it has been a retreat from the outward Datum into the personal subconscious, into a mental world more squalid and more tightly closed than even the world of conscious personality. These contraptions of tin and highly coloured plastic – where had I seen them before? In every picture gallery that exhibits the latest in non-representational art.

And now someone produced a phonograph and put a record on the turntable. I listened with pleasure, but experienced nothing comparable to my seen apocalypses of flowers or flannel. Would a naturally gifted musician *hear* the revelations which, for me, had been exclusively visual? It would be interesting to make the experiment. Meanwhile, though not transfigured, though retaining its normal quality and intensity, the music contributed not a little to my understanding of what had happened to me and of the wider problems which those happenings had raised.

Instrumental music, oddly enough, left me rather cold. Mozart's C-minor Piano Concerto was interrupted after the first movement, and a recording of some madrigals by Gesualdo took its place.

'These voices,' I said appreciatively, 'these voices – they're a kind of bridge back to the human world.'

And a bridge they remained even while singing the most startlingly chromatic of the mad prince's compositions. Through the uneven phrases of the madrigals, the music pursued its course, never sticking to the same key for two bars together. In Gesualdo, that fantastic character out of a Webster melodrama, psychological disintegration had exaggerated, had pushed, to the extreme limit, a tendency inherent in modal as opposed to fully tonal music. The resulting works sounded as though they might have been written by the later Schoenberg.

'And yet,' I felt myself constrained to say, as I listened to these strange products of a Counter-Reformation psychosis working upon a late mediaeval art form, 'and yet it does not matter that he's all in bits. The whole is disorganized. But each individual fragment is in order, is a representative of a Higher Order. The Higher Order prevails even in the disintegration. The totality is present even in the broken pieces. More clearly present, perhaps, than in a completely coherent work. At least you aren't lulled into a sense of false security by some merely human, merely fabricated order. You have to rely on your immediate perception of the ultimate order. So in a certain sense disintegration may have its advantages. But of course it's

33

dangerous, horribly dangerous. Suppose you couldn't get back, out of the chaos. ...'

From Gesualdo's madrigals we jumped, across a gulf of three centuries, to Alban Berg and the *Lyric Suite*.

'This,' I announced in advance, 'is going to be hell.'

But, as it turned out, I was wrong. Actually the music sounded rather funny. Dredged up from the personal subconscious, agony succeeded twelve-tone agony; but what struck me was only the essential incongruity between a psychological disintegration even completer than Gesualdo's and the prodigious resources, in talent and technique, employed in its expression.

'Isn't he sorry for himself?' I commented with a derisive lack of sympathy. And then, '*Katzenmusik* – learned *Katzenmusik.*' And finally, after a few more minutes of the anguish, 'Who cares what his feelings are? Why can't he pay attention to something else?'

As a criticism of what is undoubtedly a very remarkable work, it was unfair and inadequate – but not, I think, irrelevant. I cite it for what it is worth and because that is how, in a state of pure contemplation, I reacted to the *Lyric Suite*.

When it was over, the investigator suggested a walk in the garden. I was willing; and though my body seemed to have dissociated itself almost completely from my mind – or, to be more accurate, though my awareness of the transfigured outer world was no longer accompanied by an awareness of my physical organism – found myself able to get up, open the French-window and walk out with only a minimum of hesitation. It was odd, of course, to feel that 'I' was not the same as these arms and legs 'out there,' as this wholly objective trunk and neck and even head. It was odd; but one soon got used to it. And anyhow the body seemed perfectly well able to look after itself. In reality, of course, it always does look after itself. All that the conscious ego can do is to formulate wishes, which are then carried out by forces which it controls very little and understands not at all. When it does anything more – when it tries too hard, for example, when it worries, when it becomes apprehensive about the future – it lowers the effectiveness of those forces and may even cause the devitalized body to fall ill. In my present state, awareness was not referred to an ego; it was, so to speak, on its own. This meant that the physiological intelligence controlling the body was also on its own. For the moment that interfering neurotic who, in waking hours, tries to run the show was blessedly out of the way.

From the French-window I walked out under a kind of pergola covered in part by a climbing rose tree, in part by laths, one inch wide with half an inch of space between them. The sun was shining and the shadows of the laths made a zebra-like pattern on the ground and across the seat and back of a garden chair, which was standing at this end of the pergola. That chair – shall I ever forget it? Where the shadows fell on the canvas upholstery, stripes of a deep but glowing indigo alternated with stripes of an incandescence so intensely bright that it was hard to believe that they could be made of anything but blue fire. For what seemed an immensely long time I gazed without knowing, even without wishing to know, what it was that confronted me. At any other time I would have seen a chair barred with alternate light and shade. To-day the percept had swallowed up the concept. I was so completely absorbed in looking, so thunderstruck by what I actually saw, that I could not be aware of anything else.

Garden furniture, laths, sunlight, shadow – these were no more than names and notions, mere verbalizations, for utilitarian or scientific purposes, after the event. The event was this succession of azure furnace-doors separated by gulfs of unfathomable gentian. It was inexpressibly wonderful, wonderful to the point, almost, of being terrifying. And suddenly I had an inkling of what it must feel like to be mad. Schizophrenia has its heavens as well as its hells and purgatories, I remember what an old friend, dead these many years, told me about his mad wife. One day in the early stages of the disease, when she still had her lucid intervals, he had gone to the hospital to talk to her about their children. She listened for a time, then cut him short. How could he bear to waste his time on a couple of absent children, when all that really mattered, here and now, was the unspeakable beauty of the patterns he made, in this brown tweed jacket, every time he moved his arms? Alas, this paradise of cleansed perception, of pure, one-sided contemplation, was not to endure. The blissful intermissions became rarer, became briefer, until finally there were no more of them; there was only horror.

Most takers of mescalin experience only the heavenly part of schizophrenia. The drug brings hell and purgatory only to those who have had a recent case of jaundice, or who suffer from periodical depressions or a chronic anxiety. If, like the other drugs of remotely comparable power, mescalin were notoriously toxic, the taking of it would be enough, of itself, to cause anxiety. But the reasonably healthy person knows in advance that, so far as he is concerned, mescalin is completely innocuous, that its effects will pass off after eight or ten hours, leaving no hangover and consequently no craving for a renewal of the dose. Fortified by this knowledge, he embarks upon the experiment without fear – in other words, without any pre-disposition to convert an unprecedentedly strange and other than human experience into something appalling, something actually diabolical.

Confronted by a chair which looked like the Last Judgment – or, to be more accurate, by a Last Judgment which, after a long time and with considerable difficulty, I recognized as a chair – I found myself all at once on the brink of panic. This, I suddenly felt, was going too far. Too far, even though the going was into intenser beauty, deeper significance. The fear, as I analyse it in retrospect, was of being overwhelmed, of disintegrating under a pressure of reality greater than a mind, accustomed to living most of the time in a cosy world of symbols, could possibly bear. The literature of religious experience abounds in references to the pains and terrors overwhelming those who have come, too suddenly, face to face with some manifestation of the *Mysterium tremendum*. In theological language, this fear is due to the incompatibility between man's egotism and the divine purity, between man's self-aggravated separateness and the infinity of God. Following Boehme and William Law, we may say that, by unregenerate souls, the divine Light at its full blaze can be apprehended only as a burning, purgatorial fire. An almost identical doctrine is to be found in *The Tibetan Book of the Dead*, where the departed soul is described as shrinking in agony from the Clear Light of the Void, and even from the lesser, tempered Lights, in order to rush headlong into the comforting darkness of self-hood as a reborn human being, or even as a beast, an unhappy ghost, a denizen of hell. Anything rather than the burning brightness of unmitigated Reality – anything!

The schizophrenic is a soul not merely unregenerate, but desperately sick into the bargain. His sickness consists in the inability to take refuge from inner and outer reality (as the sane person habitually does) in the home-made universe of common sense – the strictly human world of useful notions, shared symbols and socially acceptable conventions. The schizophrenic is like a man permanently under the influence of mescalin, and therefore unable to shut off the experience of a reality which he is not holy enough to live with, which he cannot explain away because it is the most stubborn of primary facts, and which, because it never permits him to look at the world with merely human eyes, scares him into interpreting its unremitting strangeness, its burning intensity of significance, as the manifestations of human or even cosmic malevolence, calling for the most desperate counter-measures, from murderous violence at one end of the scale to catatonia, or psychological suicide, at the other. And once embarked upon the downward, the infernal road, one would never be able to stop. That, now, was only too obvious.

'If you started in the wrong way,' I said in answer to the investigator's questions, 'everything that happened would be a proof of the conspiracy against you. It would all be self-validating. You couldn't draw a breath without knowing it was part of the plot.'

'So you think you know where madness lies?'

My answer was a convinced and heartfelt, 'Yes.'

'And you couldn't control it?'

'No, I couldn't control it. If one began with fear and hate as the major premiss, one would have to go on to the conclusion.'

'Would you be able,' my wife asked, 'to fix your attention on what *The Tibetan Book of the Dead* calls the Clear Light?'

I was doubtful.

'Would it keep the evil away, if you could hold it? Or would you not be able to hold it?'

I considered the question for some time.

'Perhaps,' I answered at last, 'perhaps I could – but only if there were somebody there to tell me about the Clear Light. One couldn't do it by oneself. That's the point, I suppose, of the Tibetan ritual – someone sitting there all the time and telling you what's what.'

After listening to the record of this part of the experiment, I took down my copy of Evans-Wentz's edition of *The Tibetan Book of the Dead*, and opened at random. 'O nobly born, let not thy mind be distracted.' That was the problem – to remain undistracted. Undistracted by the memory of past sins, by imagined pleasure, by the bitter aftertaste of old wrongs and humiliations, by all the fears and hates and cravings that ordinarily eclipse the Light. What those Buddhist monks did for the dying and the dead, might not the modern psychiatrist do for the insane? Let there be a voice to assure them, by day and even while they are asleep, that in spite of all the terror, all the bewilderment and confusion, the ultimate Reality remains unshakably itself and is of the same substance as the inner light of even the most cruelly tormented mind. By means of such devices as recorders, clock-controlled switches, public address systems and pillow speakers it should be very easy to keep the inmates of even an understaffed institution constantly reminded of this primordial fact. Perhaps a few of the lost souls might in this way be helped to win some measure of control over the universe

— at once beautiful and appalling, but always other than human, always totally incomprehensible — in which they find themselves condemned to live.

None too soon, I was steered away from the disquieting splendours of my garden chair. Drooping in green parabolas from the hedge, the ivy fronds shone with a kind of glassy, jade-like radiance. A moment later a clump of Red Hot Pokers, in full bloom, had exploded into my field of vision. So passionately alive that they seemed to be standing on the very brink of utterance, the flowers strained upwards into the blue. Like the chair under the laths, they protested too much. I looked down at the leaves and discovered a cavernous intricacy of the most delicate green lights and shadows, pulsing with undecipherable mystery.

Roses:
The flowers are easy to paint,
The leaves difficult.

Shiki's *haiku* (which I quote in F. H. Blyth's translation) expresses, by indirection, exactly what I then felt — the excessive, the too obvious glory of the flowers, as contrasted with the subtler miracle of their foliage.

We walked out into the street. A large pale blue automobile was standing at the kerb. At the sight of it, I was suddenly overcome by enormous merriment. What complacency, what an absurd self-satisfaction beamed from those bulging surfaces of glossiest enamel! Man had created the thing in his own image — or rather in the image of his favourite character in fiction. I laughed till the tears ran down my cheeks.

We re-entered the house. A meal had been prepared. Somebody, who was not yet identical with myself, fell to with ravenous appetite. From a considerable distance and without much interest, I looked on.

When the meal had been eaten, we got into the car and went for a drive. The effects of the mescalin were already on the decline: but the flowers in the gardens still trembled on the brink of being supernatural, the pepper trees and carobs along the side streets still manifestly belonged to some sacred grove. Eden alternated with Dodona, Yggdrasil with the mystic Rose. And then, abruptly, we were at an intersection, waiting to cross Sunset Boulevard. Before us the cars were rolling by in a steady stream – thousands of them, all bright and shiny like an advertiser's dream and each more ludicrous than the last. Once again I was convulsed with laughter.

The Red Sea of traffic parted at last, and we crossed into another oasis of trees and lawns and roses. In a few minutes we had climbed to a vantage point in the hills, and there was the city spread out beneath us. Rather disappointingly, it looked very like the city I had seen on other occasions. So far as I was concerned, transfiguration was proportional to distance. The nearer, the more divinely other. This vast, dim panorama was hardly different from itself.

We drove on, and so long as we remained in the hills, with view succeeding distant view, significance was at its everyday level, well below transfiguration point. The magic began to work again only when we turned down into a new suburb and were gliding between two rows of houses. Here, in spite of the peculiar hideousness of the architecture, there were renewals of transcendental otherness, hints of the morning's heaven. Brick chimneys and green composition roofs glowed in the sunshine, like fragments of the New Jerusalem. And all at once I saw what Guardi had seen and (with what incomparable skill!) had so often rendered in his paintings – a stucco wall with a shadow slanting across it, blank but unforgettably beautiful, empty but charged with all the meaning and the mystery of existence. The Revelation dawned and was gone again within a fraction of a second. The car had moved on; time was uncovering another manifestation of the eternal Suchness. 'Within sameness there is difference. But that difference should be different from sameness is in no wise the intention of all the Buddhas. Their intention is both totality and differentiation.' This bank of red and white geraniums, for example – it was entirely different from that stucco wall a hundred yards up the road. But the 'is-ness' of both was the same, the eternal quality of their transience was the same.

An hour later, with ten more miles and the visit to the World's Biggest Drug Store safely behind us, we were back at home, and I had returned to that reassuring but profoundly unsatisfactory state known as 'being in one's right mind.'

That humanity at large will ever be able to dispense with Artificial Paradises seems very unlikely. Most men and women lead lives at the worst so painful, at the best so monotonous, poor and limited that the urge to escape, the longing to transcend themselves if only for a few moments, is and has always been one of the principal appetites of the soul. Art and religion, carnivals and saturnalia, dancing and listening to oratory – all these have served, in H. G. Wells' phrase, as Doors in the Wall. And for private, for everyday use there have always been chemical intoxicants. All the vegetable sedatives and narcotics, all the euphorics that grow on trees, the hallucinogens that ripen in berries or can be squeezed from roots – all, without exception, have been known and systematically used by human beings from time immemorial. And to these natural modifiers of consciousness modern science has added its quota of synthetics – chloral, for example, and benzedrine, the bromides and the barbiturates.

Most of these modifiers of consciousness cannot now be taken except under doctor's orders, or else illegally and at considerable risk. For unrestricted use the West has permitted only alcohol and tobacco. All the other chemical Doors in the Wall are labelled Dope, and their unauthorized takers are Fiends.

We now spend a good deal more on drink and smoke than we spend on education. This, of course, is not surprising. The urge to escape from selfhood and the environment is in almost everyone almost all the time. The urge to do something for the young is strong only in parents, and in them only for the few years during which their children go to school. Equally unsurprising is the current attitude towards drink and smoke. In spite of the growing army of hopeless alcoholics, in spite of the hundreds of thousands of persons annually maimed or killed by drunken drivers, popular comedians still crack jokes about alcohol and its addicts. And in spite of the evidence linking cigarettes with lung cancer, practically everybody regards tobacco smoking as being hardly less normal and natural than eating. From the point of view of the rationalist utilitarian this may seem odd. For the historian, it is exactly what you would expect. A firm conviction of the material reality of Hell never prevented mediaeval Christians from doing what their ambition, lust or covetousness suggested. Lung cancer, traffic accidents and the millions of miserable and misery-creating alcoholics are facts even more certain than was, in Dante's day, the fact of the Inferno. But all such facts are remote and unsubstantial compared with the near, felt fact of a craving, here and now, for release or sedation, for a drink or a smoke.

Ours is the age, among other things, of the automobile and of rocketing population. Alcohol is incompatible with safety on the roads, and its production, like that of tobacco, condemns to virtual sterility many millions of acres of the most fertile soil. The problems raised by alcohol and tobacco cannot, it goes without saying, be solved by prohibition. The universal and ever-present urge to self-transcendence is not to be abolished by slamming the currently popular Doors in the Wall. The only reasonable policy is to open other, better doors in the hope of inducing men and women to exchange their old bad habits for new and less harmful ones. Some of these other, better doors will be social and technological in nature, others religious or psychological, others dietetic, educational, athletic. But the need for frequent chemical vacations from intolerable selfhood and repulsive surroundings will undoubtedly remain. What is needed is a new drug which will relieve and console our suffering species without doing more harm in the long run than it does good in the short. Such a drug must be potent in minute doses and synthesizable. If it does not possess these qualities, its production, like that of wine, beer, spirits and tobacco will interfere with the raising of indispensable food and fibres. It must be less toxic than opium or cocaine, less likely to produce undesirable social consequences than alcohol or the barbiturates, less inimical to heart and lungs than the tars and nicotine of cigarettes. And, on the positive side, it should produce changes in consciousness more interesting, more intrinsically valuable than mere sedation or dreaminess, delusions of omnipotence or release from inhibition.

To most people, mescalin is almost completely innocuous. Unlike alcohol, it does not drive the taker into the kind of uninhibited action which results in brawls, crimes of violence and traffic accidents. A man under the influence of mescalin quietly minds his own business. Moreover, the business he minds is an experience of the most enlightening kind, which does not have to be paid for (and this is surely important) by a compensatory hangover. Of the long-range consequences of regular mescalin taking we know very little. The Indians who consume peyote buttons do not seem to be physically or morally degraded by the habit. However, the available evidence is still scarce and sketchy.[1]

Although obviously superior to cocaine, opium,

[1] In his monograph *Menomini Peyotism*, published (December 1952) in the Transactions of the American Philosophical Society, Professor J. S. Slotkin has written that 'the habitual use of Peyote does not seem to produce any increased tolerance or dependence. I know many people who have been Peyotists for forty to fifty years. The amount of Peyote they use depends upon the solemnity of the occasion; in general they do not take any more Peyote now than they did years ago. Also, there is sometimes an interval of a month or more between rites, and they go without Peyote during this period without feeling any craving for it. Personally, even after a series of rites occurring on four successive weekends, I neither increased the amount of Peyote consumed nor felt any continued need for it.' It is evidently with good reason that 'Peyote has never been legally declared a narcotic, or its use prohibited by the federal government.' However, 'during the long history of Indian-white contact, white officials have usually tried to suppress the use of Peyote, because it has been conceived to violate their own mores. But these attempts have always failed.' In a footnote Dr Slotkin adds that 'it is amazing to hear the fantastic stories about the effects of Peyote and the nature of the ritual, which are told by the white and Catholic Indian officials in the Menomini Reservation. None of them have had the slightest first-hand experience with the plant or with the religion, yet some fancy themselves to be authorities and write official reports on the subject.'

alcohol and tobacco, mescalin is not yet the ideal drug. Along with the happily transfigured majority of mescalin takers there is a minority that finds in the drug only hell or purgatory. Moreover, for a drug that is to be used, like alcohol, for general consumption, its effects last for an inconveniently long time. But chemistry and physiology are capable nowadays of practically anything. If the psychologists and sociologists will define the ideal, the neurologists and pharmacologists can be relied upon to discover the means whereby that ideal can be realized or at least (for perhaps this kind of ideal can never, in the very nature of things, be fully realized) more nearly approached than in the wine-bibbing past, the whisky-drinking, marijuana-smoking and barbiturate-swallowing present.

The urge to transcend self-conscious selfhood is, as I have said, a principal appetite of the soul. When, for whatever reason, men and women fail to transcend themselves by means of worship, good works and spiritual exercises, they are apt to resort to religion's chemical surrogates – alcohol and 'goof-pills' in the modern West, alcohol and opium in the East, hashish in the Mohammedan world, alcohol and marijuana in Central America, alcohol and coca in the Andes, alcohol and the barbiturates in the more up-to-date regions of South America. In *Poisons Sacrés, Ivresses Divines* Philippe de Félice has written at length and with a wealth of documentation on the immemorial connection between religion and the taking of drugs. Here, in summary or in direct quotation, are his conclusions. The employment for religious purposes of toxic substances is 'extraordinarily widespread. . . . The practices studied in this volume can be observed in every region of the earth, among primitives no less than among those who have reached a high pitch of civilization. We are therefore dealing not with exceptional facts, which might justifiably be overlooked, but with a general and, in the widest sense of the word, a human phenomenon, the kind of phenomenon which cannot be disregarded by anyone who is trying to discover what religion is, and what are the deep needs which it must satisfy.'

Ideally, everyone should be able to find self-transcendence in some form of pure or applied religion. In practice it seems very unlikely that this hoped for consummation will ever be realized. There are, and doubtless there always will be, good churchmen and good churchwomen for whom, unfortunately, piety is not enough. The late G. K. Chesterton, who wrote at least as lyrically of drink as of devotion, may serve as their eloquent spokesman.

The modern Churches, with some exceptions among the Protestant denominations, tolerate alcohol; but even the most tolerant have made no attempt to convert the drug to Christianity, or to sacramentalize its use. The pious drinker is forced to take his religion in one compartment, his religion-surrogate in another. And perhaps this is inevitable. Drinking cannot be sacramentalized except in religions which set no store on decorum. The worship of Dionysos or the Celtic god of beer was a loud and disorderly affair. The rites of Christianity are incompatible with even religious drunkenness. This does no harm to the distillers, but is very bad for Christianity. Countless persons desire self-transcendence and would be glad to find it in church. But, alas, 'the hungry sheep look up and are not fed.' They take part in rites, they listen to sermons, they repeat prayers; but their thirst remains unassuaged.

Disappointed, they turn to the bottle. For a time at least and in a kind of way, it works. Church may still be attended; but it is no more than the Musical Bank of Butler's *Erewhon*. God may still be acknowledged; but He is God only on the verbal level, only in a strictly Pickwickian sense. The effective object of worship is the bottle and the sole religious experience is that state of uninhibited and belligerent euphoria which follows the ingestion of the third cocktail.

We see, then, that Christianity and alcohol do not and cannot mix. Christianity and mescalin seem to be much more compatible. This has been demonstrated by many tribes of Indians, from Texas to as far north as Wisconsin. Among these tribes are to be found groups affiliated with the Native American Church, a sect whose principal rite is a kind of Early Christian Agape, or Love-Feast, where slices of peyote take the place of the sacramental bread and wine. These Native Americans regard the cactus as God's special gift to the Indians, and equate its effects with the workings of the divine Spirit.

Professor J. S. Slotkin – one of the very few white men ever to have participated in the rites of a Peyotist congregation – says of his fellow worshippers that they are 'certainly not stupefied or drunk. . . . They never get out of rhythm or fumble their words, as a drunken or stupefied man would do. . . . They are all quiet, courteous and considerate of one another. I have never been in any white man's house of worship where there is either so much religious feeling or decorum.' And what, we may ask, are these devout and well-behaved Peyotists experiencing? Not the mild sense of virtue which sustains the average Sunday churchgoer through ninety minutes of boredom. Not even those high feelings, inspired by thoughts of the Creator and the Redeemer, the Judge and the Comforter, which animate the pious. For these Native Americans, religious experience is something more direct and illuminating, more spontaneous, less the home-made product of the superficial, self-conscious mind. Sometimes (according to the reports collected by Dr Slotkin) they see visions, which may be of Christ Himself. Sometimes they hear the voice of the Great Spirit. Sometimes they become aware of the presence of God and of those personal shortcomings which must be corrected if they are to do His will. The practical consequences of these chemical openings of doors into the Other World seem to be wholly good. Dr Slotkin reports that habitual Peyotists are on the whole more industrious, more temperate (many of them abstain altogether from alcohol), more peaceable than non-Peyotists. A tree with such satisfactory fruits cannot be condemned out of hand as evil.

In sacramentalizing the use of peyote, the Indians of the Native American Church have done something which is at once psychologically sound and historically respectable. In the early centuries of Christianity many pagan rites and festivals were baptized, so to say, and made to serve the purposes of the Church. These jollifications were not particularly edifying; but they assuaged a certain psychological hunger and, instead of trying to suppress them, the earlier missionaries had the sense to accept them for what they were, soul-satisfying expressions of fundamental urges, and to incorporate them into the fabric of the new religion. What the Native Americans have done is essentially similar. They have taken a pagan custom (a custom, incidentally, far more elevating and enlightening than most of the rather brutish carousals and mummeries adopted from European paganism) and given it a Christian significance.

Though but recently introduced into the northern United States, peyote-eating and the religion based upon it have become important symbols of the Red Man's right to spiritual independence. Some Indians have reacted to white supremacy by becoming Americanized, others by retreating into traditional Indianism. But some have tried to make the best of both worlds, indeed of all the worlds – the best of Indianism, the best of Christianity, and the best of those Other Worlds of transcendental experience, where the soul knows itself as unconditioned and of like nature with the divine. Hence the Native American Church. In it two great appetites of the soul – the urge to independence and self-determination and the urge to self-transcendence – were fused with, and interpreted in the light of, a third – the urge to worship, to justify the ways of God to man, to explain the universe by means of a coherent theology.

Lo, the poor Indian, whose untutored mind
Clothes him in front, but leaves him bare behind.

But actually it is we, the rich and highly educated whites, who have left ourselves bare behind. We cover our anterior nakedness with some philosophy – Christian, Marxian, Freudo-Physicalist – but abaft we remain uncovered, at the mercy of all the winds of circumstance. The poor Indian, on the other hand, has had the wit to protect his rear by supplementing the fig-leaf of a theology with the breech-clout of transcendental experience.

I am not so foolish as to equate what happens under the influence of mescalin or of any other drug, prepared or in the future preparable, with the realization of the end and ultimate purpose of human life: Enlightenment, the Beatific Vision. All I am suggesting is that the mescalin experience is what Catholic theologians call 'a gratuitous grace,' not necessary to salvation but potentially helpful and to be accepted thankfully, if made available. To be shaken out of the ruts of ordinary perception, to be shown for a few timeless hours the outer and the inner world, not as they appear to an animal obsessed with survival or to a human being obsessed with words and notions, but as they are apprehended, directly and unconditionally, by Mind at Large – this is an experience of inestimable value to everyone and especially to the intellectual. For the intellectual is by definition the man for whom, in Goethe's phrase, 'the word is essentially fruitful.' He is the man who feels that 'what we perceive by the eye is foreign to us as such and need not impress us deeply.' And yet, though himself an intellectual and one of the supreme masters of language, Goethe did not always agree with his own evaluation of the word. 'We talk,' he wrote in middle life, 'far too much. We should talk less and draw more. I personally should like to renounce speech altogether and, like organic Nature, communicate everything I have to say in sketches. That fig tree, this little snake, the cocoon on my window sill quietly awaiting its future – all these are momentous signatures. A person able to decipher their meaning properly would soon be able to dispense with the written or the spoken word altogether. The more I think of it, there is something futile, mediocre, even (I am tempted to say) foppish about speech. By contrast, how the gravity of Nature and her silence startle you, when you stand face to face with her, undistracted, before a barren ridge or in the desolation of the ancient hills.' We can never dispense with language and the other symbol systems; for it is by means of them, and only by their means, that we have raised ourselves above the brutes, to the level of human beings. But we can easily become the victims as well as the beneficiaries of these systems. We must learn how to handle words effectively; but at the same time we must preserve and, if necessary, intensify our ability to look at the world directly and not through that half-opaque medium of concepts, which distorts every given fact into the all too familiar likeness of some generic label or explanatory abstraction.

Literary or scientific, liberal or specialist, all our education is predominantly verbal and therefore fails to accomplish what it is supposed to do. Instead of transforming children into fully developed adults, it turns out students of the natural sciences who are completely unaware of Nature as the primary fact of experience, it inflicts upon the world students of the Humanities who know nothing of humanity, their own or anyone else's.

Gestalt psychologists, such as Samuel Renshaw, have devised methods for widening the range and increasing the acuity of human perceptions. But do our educators apply them? The answer is, No.

Teachers in every field of psycho-physical skill, from seeing to tennis, from tightrope walking to prayer, have discovered, by trial and error, the conditions of optimum functioning within their special fields. But have any of the great Foundations financed a project for co-ordinating these empirical findings into a general theory and practice of heightened creativeness? Again, so far as I am aware, the answer is, No.

All sorts of cultists and queer fish teach all kinds of techniques for achieving health, contentment, peace of mind; and for many of their hearers many of these techniques are demonstrably effective. But do we see respectable psychologists, philosophers and clergymen boldly descending into those odd and sometimes malodorous wells, at the bottom of which poor Truth is so often condemned to sit? Yet once more the answer is, No.

And now look at the history of mescalin research. Seventy years ago men of first-rate ability described the transcendental experiences which come to those who, in good health, under proper conditions and in the right spirit, take the drug. How many philosophers, how many theologians, how many professional educators have had the curiosity to open this Door in the Wall? The answer, for all practical purposes, is, None.

In a world where education is predominantly verbal, highly educated people find it all but impossible to pay serious attention to anything but words and notions. There is always money for, there are always doctorates in, the learned foolery of research into what, for scholars, is the all-important problem: Who influenced whom to say what when? Even in this age of technology the verbal Humanities are honoured. The nonverbal Humanities, the arts of being directly aware of the given facts of our existence, are almost completely ignored. A catalogue, a bibliography, a definitive edition of a third-rate versifier's *ipsissima verba*, a stupendous index to end all indexes – any genuinely Alexandrian project is sure of approval and financial support. But when it comes to finding out how you and I, our children and grandchildren, may become more perceptive, more intensely aware of inward and outward reality, more open to the Spirit, less apt, by psychological malpractices, to make ourselves physically ill, and more capable of controlling our own autonomic nervous system – when it comes to any form of non-verbal education more fundamental (and more likely to be of some practical use) than Swedish Drill, no really respectable person in any really respectable university or church will do anything about it. Verbalists are suspicious of the non-verbal; rationalists fear the given, non-rational fact; intellectuals feel that 'what we perceive by the eye (or in any other way) is foreign to us as such and need not impress us deeply.' Besides, this matter of education in the non-verbal Humanities will not fit into any of the established pigeon-holes. It is not religion, not neurology, not gymnastics, not morality or civics, not even experimental psychology. This being so, the subject is, for academic and ecclesiastical purposes, non-existent and may safely be ignored altogether or left, with a patronizing smile, to those whom the Pharisees of verbal orthodoxy call cranks, quacks, charlatans and unqualified amateurs.

'I have always found,' Blake wrote rather bitterly, 'that Angels have the vanity to speak of themselves as the only wise. This they do with a confident insolence sprouting from systematic reasoning.'

Systematic reasoning is something we could not, as a species or as individuals, possibly do without. But neither, if we are to remain sane, can we possibly do without direct perception, the more unsystematic the better, of the inner and outer worlds into which we have been born. This given reality is an infinite which passes all understanding and yet admits of being directly and in some sort totally apprehended. It is a transcendence belonging to another order than the human, and yet it may be present to us as a felt immanence, an experienced participation. To be enlightened is to be aware, always, of total reality in its immanent otherness – to be aware of it and yet to remain in a condition to survive as an animal, to think and feel as a human being, to resort whenever expedient to systematic reasoning. Our goal is to discover that we have always been where we ought to be. Unhappily we make the task exceedingly difficult for ourselves. Meanwhile, however, there are gratuitous graces in the form of partial and fleeting realizations. Under a more realistic, a less exclusively verbal system of education than ours, every Angel (in Blake's sense of that word) would be permitted as a sabbatical treat, would be urged and even, if necessary, compelled to take an occasional trip through some chemical Door in the Wall into the world of transcendental experience. If it terrified him, it would be unfortunate but probably salutary. If it brought him a brief but timeless illumination, so much the better. In either case the Angel might lose a little of the confident insolence sprouting from systematic reasoning and the consciousness of having read all the books.

Near the end of his life Aquinas experienced Infused Contemplation. Thereafter he refused to go back to work on his unfinished book. Compared with *this*, everything he had read and argued about and written – Aristotle and the Sentences, the Questions, the Propositions, the majestic Summas – was no better than chaff or straw. For most intellectuals such a sit-down strike would be inadvisable, even morally wrong. But the Angelic Doctor had done more systematic reasoning than any twelve ordinary Angels, and was already ripe for death. He had earned the right, in those last months of his mortality, to turn from merely symbolic straw and chaff to the bread of actual and substantial Fact. For Angels of a lower order and with better prospects of longevity, there must be a return to the straw. But the man who comes back through the Door in the Wall will never be quite the same as the man who went out. He will be wiser but less cocksure, happier but less self-satisfied, humbler in acknowledging his ignorance yet better equipped to understand the relationship of words to things, of systematic reasoning to the unfathomable Mystery which it tries, forever vainly, to comprehend.

HEAVEN AND HELL

Foreword

This little book is a sequel to *The Doors of Perception*. For a person in whom 'the candle of vision' never burns spontaneously, the mescalin experience is doubly illuminating. It throws light on the hitherto unknown regions of his own mind; and at the same time it throws light, indirectly, on other minds, more richly gifted in respect to vision than his own. Reflecting on his experience, he comes to a new and better understanding of the ways in which those other minds perceive and feel and think, of the cosmological notions which seem to them self-evident, and of the works of art through which they feel impelled to express themselves. In what follows I have tried to set down, more or less systematically, the results of this new understanding.

A. H.

Heaven and Hell

In the history of science the collector of specimens preceded the zoologist and followed the exponents of natural theology and magic. He had ceased to study animals in the spirit of the authors of the Bestiaries, for whom the ant was incarnate industry, the panther an emblem, surprisingly enough, of Christ, the polecat a shocking example of uninhibited lasciviousness. But, except in a rudimentary way, he was not yet a physiologist, ecologist or student of animal behaviour. His primary concern was to make a census, to catch, kill, stuff and describe as many kinds of beasts as he could lay his hands on.

Like the earth of a hundred years ago, our mind still has its darkest Africas, its unmapped Borneos and Amazonian basins. In relation to the fauna of these regions we are not yet zoologists, we are mere naturalists and collectors of specimens. The fact is unfortunate; but we have to accept it, we have to make the best of it. However lowly, the work of the collector must be done, before we can proceed to the higher scientific tasks of classification, analysis, experiment and theory making.

Like the giraffe and the duck-billed platypus, the creatures inhabiting these remoter regions of the mind are exceedingly improbable. Nevertheless they exist, they are facts of observation; and as such, they cannot be ignored by anyone who is honestly trying to understand the world in which he lives.

It is difficult, it is all but impossible, to speak of mental events except in similes drawn from the more familiar universe of material things. If I have made use of geographical and zoological metaphors, it is not wantonly, out of a mere addiction to picturesque language. It is because such metaphors express very forcibly the essential otherness of the mind's far continents, the complete autonomy and self-sufficiency of their inhabitants. A man consists of what I may call an Old World of personal consciousness and, beyond a dividing sea, a series of New Worlds – the not too distant Virginias and Carolinas of the personal subconscious and the vegetative soul; the Far West of the collective unconscious, with its flora of symbols, its tribes of aboriginal archetypes; and, across another, vaster ocean, at the antipodes of everyday consciousness, the world of Visionary Experience.

If you go to New South Wales, you will see marsupials hopping about the countryside. And if you go to the antipodes of the self-conscious mind, you will encounter all sorts of creatures at least as odd as kangaroos. You do not invent these creatures any more than you invent marsupials. They live their own lives in complete independence. A man cannot control them. All he can do is to go to the mental equivalent of Australia and look around him.

Some people never consciously discover their antipodes. Others make an occasional landing. Yet others (but they are few) find it easy to go and come as they please. For the naturalist of the mind, the collector of psychological specimens, the primary need is some safe, easy and reliable method of transporting himself and others from the Old World to the New, from the continent of familiar cows and horses to the continent of the wallaby and the platypus.

Two such methods exist. Neither of them is perfect;

but both are sufficiently reliable, sufficiently easy and sufficiently safe to justify their employment by those who know what they are doing. In the first case the soul is transported to its far-off destination by the aid of a chemical – either mescalin or lysergic acid. In the second case, the vehicle is psychological in nature, and the passage to the mind's antipodes is accomplished by hypnosis. The two vehicles carry the consciousness to the same region; but the drug has the longer range and takes its passengers further into the *terra incognita*.[1]

How and why does hypnosis produce its observed effects? We do not know. For our present purposes, however, we do not have to know. All that is necessary, in this context, is to record the fact that some hypnotic subjects are transported, in the trance state, to a region in the mind's antipodes, where they find the equivalent of marsupials – strange psychological creatures leading an autonomous existence according to the law of their own being.

About the physiological effects of mescalin we know a little. Probably (for we are not yet certain) it interferes with the enzyme system that regulates cerebral functioning. By doing so it lowers the efficiency of the brain as an instrument for focusing mind on the problems of life on the surface of our planet. This lowering of what may be called the biological efficiency of the brain seems to permit the entry into consciousness of certain classes of mental events, which are normally excluded, because they possess no survival value. Similar intrusions of biologically useless, but aesthetically and sometimes spiritually valuable material may occur as the result of illness or fatigue; or they may be

[1] See Appendix I.

induced by fasting, or a period of confinement in a place of darkness and complete silence.[1]

A person under the influence of mescalin or lysergic acid will stop seeing visions when given a large dose of nicotinic acid. This helps to explain the effectiveness of fasting as an inducer of visionary experience. By reducing the amount of available sugar, fasting lowers the brain's biological efficiency and so makes possible the entry into consciousness of material possessing no survival value. Moreover, by causing a vitamin deficiency, it removes from the blood that known inhibitor of visions, nicotinic acid. Another inhibitor of visionary experience is ordinary, everyday, perceptual experience. Experimental psychologists have found that, if you confine a man to a 'restricted environment,' where there is no light, no sound, nothing to smell and, if you put him in a tepid bath with only one, almost imperceptible thing to touch, the victim will very soon start 'seeing things,' 'hearing things' and having strange bodily sensations.

Milarepa, in his Himalayan cavern, and the anchorites of the Thebaid followed essentially the same procedure and got essentially the same results. A thousand pictures of the Temptations of St Anthony bear witness to the effectiveness of restricted diet and restricted environment. Asceticism, it is evident, has a double motivation. If men and women torment their bodies, it is not only because they hope in this way to atone for past sins and avoid future punishments; it is also because they long to visit the mind's antipodes and do some visionary sightseeing. Empirically and from the reports of other ascetics, they know that fasting and a restricted environment will transport them where they

[1] See Appendix II.

long to go. Their self-inflicted punishment may be the door to paradise. (It may also – and this is a point which will be discussed in a later paragraph – be a door into the infernal regions.)

From the point of view of an inhabitant of the Old World, marsupials are exceedingly odd. But oddity is not the same as randomness. Kangaroos and wallabies may lack verisimilitude; but their improbability repeats itself and obeys recognizable laws. The same is true of the psychological creatures inhabiting the remoter regions of our minds. The experiences encountered under · the influence of mescalin or deep hypnosis are certainly strange; but they are strange with a certain regularity, strange according to a pattern.

What are the common features which this pattern imposes upon our visionary experiences? First and most important is the experience of light. Everything seen by those who visit the mind's antipodes is brilliantly illuminated and seems to shine from within. All colours are intensified to a pitch far beyond anything seen in the normal state, and at the same time the mind's capacity for recognizing fine distinctions of tone and hue is notably heightened.

In this respect there is a marked difference between these visionary experiences and ordinary dreams. Most dreams are without colour, or else are only partially or feebly coloured. On the other hand, the visions met with under the influence of mescalin or hypnosis are always intensely and, one might say, praeternaturally brilliant in colour. Professor Calvin Hall, who has collected records of many thousands of dreams, tells us that about two-thirds of all dreams are in black and white. 'Only one dream in three is coloured, or has some colour in it.' A few people dream entirely in colour; a few never experience colour in their dreams; the majority sometimes dream in colour, but more often do not.

'We have come to the conclusion,' writes Dr Hall, 'that colour in dreams yields no information about the personality of the dreamer.' I agree with this conclusion. Colour in dreams and visions tells us no more about the personality of the beholder than does colour in the external world. A garden in July is perceived as brightly coloured. The perception tells us something about sunshine, flowers and butterflies, but little or nothing about our own selves. In the same way the fact that we see brilliant colours in our visions and in some of our dreams tells us something about the fauna of the mind's antipodes, but nothing whatever about the personality who inhabits what I have called the Old World of the mind.

Most dreams are concerned with the dreamer's private wishes and instinctive urges, and with the conflicts which arise when these wishes and urges are thwarted by a disapproving conscience or a fear of public opinion. The story of these drives and conflicts is told in terms of dramatic symbols, and in most dreams the symbols are uncoloured. Why should this be the case? The answer, I presume, is that, to be effective, symbols do not require to be coloured. The letters in which we write about roses need not be red, and we can describe the rainbow by means of ink marks on white paper. Textbooks are illustrated by line engravings and half-tone plates; and these uncoloured images and diagrams effectively convey information.

What is good enough for the waking consciousness is evidently good enough for the personal subconscious, which finds it possible to express its meanings through uncoloured symbols. Colour turns out to be a kind of touchstone of reality. That which is given is coloured; that which our symbol-creating intellect and fancy put together is uncoloured. Thus the external world is perceived as coloured. Dreams, which are not given but fabricated by the personal subconscious, are generally in black and white. (It is worth remarking that, in most people's experience, the most brightly coloured dreams are those of landscapes, in which there is no drama, no symbolic reference to conflict, merely the presentation to consciousness of a given, non-human fact.)

The images of the archetypal world are symbolic; but since we, as individuals, do not fabricate them, but find them 'out there' in the collective unconscious, they exhibit some at least of the characteristics of given reality and are coloured. The non-symbolic inhabitants of the mind's antipodes exist in their own right, and like the given facts of the external world are coloured. Indeed, they are far more intensely coloured than external data. This may be explained, at least in part, by the fact that our perceptions of the external world are habitually clouded by the verbal notions in terms of which we do our thinking. We are for ever attempting to convert things into signs for the more intelligible abstractions of our own invention. But in doing so, we rob these things of a great deal of their native thinghood.

At the antipodes of the mind, we are more or less completely free of language, outside the system of conceptual thought. Consequently our perception of visionary objects possesses all the freshness, all the naked intensity, of experiences which have never been verbalized, never assimilated to lifeless abstractions. Their colour (that hallmark of givenness) shines forth with a brilliance which seems to us praeternatural, because it is in fact entirely natural – entirely natural in the sense of being entirely unsophisticated by language or the scientific, philosophical and utilitarian notions, by means of which we ordinarily re-create the given world in our own drearily human image.

In his *Candle of Vision*, the Irish poet A. E. (George Russell) has analysed his visionary experiences with remarkable acuity. 'When I meditate,' he writes, 'I feel in the thoughts and images that throng about me the reflections of personality; but there are also windows in the soul, through which can be seen images created not by human but by the divine imagination.'

Our linguistic habits lead us into error. For example, we are apt to say, 'I imagine,' when what we should have said is, 'The curtain was lifted that I might see.' Spontaneous or induced, visions are never our personal property. Memories belonging to the ordinary self have no place in them. The things seen are wholly un-familiar. 'There is no reference or resemblance,' in Sir William Herschel's phrase, 'to any objects recently seen or even thought of.' When faces appear, they are never the faces of friends or acquaintances. We are out of the Old World, and exploring the antipodes.

For most of us most of the time, the world of every-day experience seems rather dim and drab. But for a few people often, and for a fair number occasionally, some of the brightness of visionary experience spills over, as it were, into common seeing, and the everyday universe is transfigured. Though still recognizably itself, the Old World takes on the quality of the mind's antipodes. Here is an entirely characteristic description of this transfiguration of the everyday world.

'I was sitting on the seashore, half listening to a friend arguing violently about something which merely bored me. Unconsciously to myself, I looked at a film of sand I had picked up on my hand, when I suddenly saw the exquisite beauty of every little grain of it; instead of being dull, I saw that each particle was made up on a perfect geometrical pattern, with sharp angles, from each of which a brilliant shaft of light was reflected, while each tiny crystal shone like a rainbow. ... The rays crossed and recrossed, making exquisite patterns of such beauty that they left me breathless. ... Then, suddenly, my consciousness was lighted up from within and I saw in a vivid way how the whole universe was made up of particles of material which, no matter how dull and lifeless they might seem, were nevertheless filled with this intense and vital beauty. For a second or two the whole world appeared as a blaze of glory. When it died down, it left me with something I have never forgotten and which constantly reminds me of the beauty locked up in every minute speck of material around us.'

Similarly George Russell writes of seeing the world illumined by 'an intolerable lustre of light'; of finding himself looking at 'landscapes as lovely as a lost Eden'; of beholding a world where the 'colours were brighter and purer, and yet made a softer harmony.' Again, 'the winds were sparkling and diamond clear, and yet full of colour as an opal, as they glittered through the valley, and I knew the Golden Age was all about me, and it was we who had been blind to it, but that it had never passed away from the world.'

Many similar descriptions are to be found in the poets and in the literature of religious mysticism. One thinks, for example, of Wordsworth's *Ode on the Inti-*

mations of Immortality in Early Childhood; of certain lyrics by George Herbert and Henry Vaughan; of Traherne's *Centuries of Meditations*; of the passage in his autobiography, where Father Surin describes the miraculous transformation of an enclosed convent garden into a fragment of heaven.

Praeternatural light and colour are common to all visionary experiences. And along with light and colour there goes, in every case, a recognition of heightened significance. The self-luminous objects which we see in the mind's antipodes possess a meaning, and this meaning is, in some sort, as intense as their colour. Significance here is identical with being; for, at the mind's antipodes, objects do not stand for anything but themselves. The images which appear in the nearer reaches of the collective subconscious have meaning in relation to the basic facts of human experience; but here, at the limits of the visionary world, we are confronted by facts which, like the facts of external nature, are independent of man, both individually and collectively, and exist in their own right. And their meaning consists precisely in this, that they are intensely themselves and, being intensely themselves, are manifestations of the essential givenness, the non-human otherness of the universe.

Light, colour and significance do not exist in isolation. They modify, or are manifested by, objects. Are there any special classes of objects common to most visionary experiences? The answer is: Yes, there are. Under mescalin and hypnosis, as well as in spontaneous visions, certain classes of perceptual experiences turn up again and again.

The typical mescalin or lysergic acid experience

70

begins with perceptions of coloured, moving, living geometrical forms. In time, pure geometry becomes concrete, and the visionary perceives, not patterns, but patterned things, such as carpets, carvings, mosaics. These give place to vast and complicated buildings, in the midst of landscapes, which change continuously, passing from richness to more intensely coloured richness, from grandeur to deepening grandeur. Heroic figures, of the kind that Blake called 'The Seraphim,' may make their appearance, alone or in multitudes. Fabulous animals move across the scene. Everything is novel and amazing. Almost never does the visionary see anything that reminds him of his own past. He is not remembering scenes, persons or objects, and he is not inventing them; he is looking on at a new creation.

The raw material for this creation is provided by the visual experiences of ordinary life; but the moulding of this material into forms is the work of someone who is most certainly not the self, who originally had the experiences, or who later recalled and reflected upon them. They are (to quote the words used by Dr J. R. Smythies in a recent paper in the *American Journal of Psychiatry*) 'the work of a highly differentiated mental compartment, without any apparent connection, emotional or volitional, with the aims, interests, or feelings of the person concerned.'

Here, in quotation or condensed paraphrase, is Weir Mitchell's account of the visionary world to which he was transported by peyote, the cactus which is the natural source of mescalin.

At his entry into that world he saw a host of 'star points' and what looked like 'fragments of stained glass.' Then came 'delicate floating films of colour.' These were displaced by an 'abrupt rush of countless

71

points of white light,' sweeping across the field of vision. Next there were zigzag lines of very bright colours, which somehow turned into swelling clouds of still more brilliant hues. Buildings now made their appearance, and then landscapes. There was a Gothic tower of elaborate design with worn statues in the doorways or on stone brackets. 'As I gazed, every projecting angle, cornice and even the faces of the stones at their joinings were by degrees covered or hung with clusters of what seemed to be huge precious stones, but uncut stones, some being more like masses of transparent fruit. ... All seemed to possess an interior light.' The Gothic tower gave place to a mountain, a cliff of inconceivable height, a colossal birdclaw carved in stone and projecting over the abyss, an endless unfurling of coloured draperies, and an efflorescence of more precious stones. Finally there was a view of green and purple waves breaking on a beach 'with myriads of lights of the same tint as the waves.'

Every mescalin experience, every vision arising under hypnosis, is unique; but all recognizably belong to the same species. The landscapes, the architectures, the clustering gems, the brilliant and intricate patterns – these, in their atmosphere of praeternatural light, praeternatural colour and praeternatural significance, are the stuff of which the mind's antipodes are made. Why this should be so, we have no idea. It is a brute fact of experience which, whether we like it or not, we have to accept – just as we have to accept the fact of kangaroos.

From these facts of visionary experience let us now pass to the accounts preserved in all the cultural traditions, of Other Worlds – the worlds inhabited by the gods, by the spirits of the dead, by man in his primal state of innocence.

Reading these accounts, we are immediately struck by the close similarity between induced or spontaneous visionary experience and the heavens and fairylands of folklore and religion. Praeternatural light, praeternatural intensity of colouring, praeternatural significance – these are characteristic of all the Other Worlds and Golden Ages. And in virtually every case this praeternaturally significant light shines on, or shines out of, a landscape of such surpassing beauty that words cannot express it.

Thus in the Graeco-Roman tradition we find the lovely Garden of the Hesperides, the Elysian Plain, and the fair Island of Leuke, to which Achilles was translated. Memnon went to another luminous island, somewhere in the East. Odysseus and Penelope travelled in the opposite direction and enjoyed their immortality with Circe in Italy. Still further to the West were the Islands of the Blest, first mentioned by Hesiod and so firmly believed in that, as late as the first century B.C., Sertorius planned to send a squadron from Spain to discover them.

Magically lovely islands reappear in the folklore of the Celts and, at the opposite side of the world, in that of the Japanese. And between Avalon in the extreme West and Horaisan in the Far East, there is the land of Uttarakuru, the Other World of the Hindus. 'The land,' we read in the *Ramayana*, 'is watered by lakes with golden lotuses. There are rivers by thousands, full of leaves of the colour of sapphire and lapis lazuli; and the lakes, resplendent like the morning sun, are adorned by golden beds of red lotus. The country all around is covered by jewels and precious stones, with gay beds of blue lotus, golden-petalled. Instead of sand, pearls, gems and gold form the banks of the rivers, which are overhung with trees of fire-bright gold. These trees perpetually bear flowers and fruit, give forth a sweet fragrance and abound with birds.'

Uttarakuru, we see, resembles the landscapes of the mescalin experience in being rich with precious stones. And this characteristic is common to virtually all the Other Worlds of religious tradition. Every paradise abounds in gems, or at least in gem-like objects resembling, as Weir Mitchell puts it, 'transparent fruit.' Here, for example, is Ezekiel's version of the Garden of Eden. 'Thou hast been in Eden, the garden of God. Every precious stone was thy covering, the sardius, topaz and the diamond, the beryl, the onyx and the jasper, the sapphire, the emerald and the carbuncle, and gold. . . . Thou art the anointed cherub that covereth . . . thou hast walked up and down in the midst of the stones of fire.' The Buddhist paradises are adorned with similar 'stones of fire.' Thus, the Western Paradise of the Pure Land Sect is walled with silver, gold and beryl; has lakes with jewelled banks and a profusion of glowing lotuses, within which the Bodhisattvas sit enthroned.

In describing their Other Worlds, the Celts and Teutons speak very little of precious stones, but have much to say of another and, for them, equally wonderful substance – glass. The Welsh had a blessed land called Ynisvitrin, the Isle of Glass; and one of the names of the Germanic kingdom of the dead was Glasberg. One is reminded of the Sea of Glass in the Apocalypse.

Most paradises are adorned with buildings, and, like

the trees, the waters, the hills and fields, these buildings are bright with gems. We are all familiar with the New Jerusalem, 'And the building of the wall of it was of jasper, and the city was of pure gold, like unto clear glass. And the foundations of the wall of the city were garnished with all manner of precious stones.'

Similar descriptions are to be found in the eschatological literature of Hinduism, Buddhism and Islam. Heaven is always a place of gems. Why should this be the case? Those who think of all human activities in terms of a social and economic frame of reference will give some such answer as this: Gems are very rare on earth. Few people possess them. To compensate themselves for these facts, the spokesmen for the poverty-stricken majority have filled their imaginary heavens with precious stones. This 'pie in the sky' hypothesis contains, no doubt, some element of truth; but it fails to explain why precious stones should have come to be regarded as precious in the first place.

Men have spent enormous amounts of time, energy and money on the finding, mining and cutting of coloured pebbles. Why? The utilitarian can offer no explanation for such fantastic behaviour. But as soon as we take into account the facts of visionary experience, everything becomes clear. In vision, men perceive a profusion of what Ezekiel calls 'stones of fire,' of what Weir Mitchell describes as 'transparent fruit.' These things are self-luminous, exhibit a praeternatural brilliance of colour and possess a praeternatural significance. The material objects which most nearly resemble these sources of visionary illumination are gem-stones. To acquire such a stone is to acquire something whose preciousness is guaranteed by the fact that it exists in the Other World.

Hence man's otherwise inexplicable passion for gems and hence his attribution to precious stones of therapeutic and magical virtue. The causal chain, I am convinced, begins in the psychological Other World of visionary experience, descends to earth and mounts again to the theological Other World of heaven. In this context the words of Socrates, in the *Phaedo*, take on a new significance. There exists, he tells us, an ideal world above and beyond the world of matter. 'In this other earth the colours are much purer and much more brilliant than they are down here.... The very mountains, the very stones have a richer gloss, a lovelier transparency and intensity of hue. The precious stones of this lower world, our highly prized cornelians, jaspers, emeralds and all the rest, are but the tiny fragments of these stones above. In the other earth there is no stone but is precious and exceeds in beauty every gem of ours.'

In other words, precious stones are precious because they bear a faint resemblance to the glowing marvels seen with the inner eye of the visionary. 'The view of that world,' says Plato, 'is a vision of blessed beholders'; for to see things 'as they are in themselves' is bliss unalloyed and inexpressible.

Among people who have no knowledge of precious stones or of glass, heaven is adorned not with minerals, but flowers. Praeternaturally brilliant flowers bloom in most of the Other Worlds described by primitive eschatologists, and even in the begemmed and glassy paradises of the more advanced religions they have their place. One remembers the lotus of Hindu and Buddhist tradition, the roses and lilies of the West.

'God first planted a garden.' The statement expresses a deep psychological truth. Horticulture has its source –

or at any rate one of its sources – in the Other World of the mind's antipodes. When worshippers offer flowers at the altar, they are returning to the gods things which they know, or (if they are not visionaries) obscurely feel, to be indigenous to heaven.

And this return to the source is not merely symbolical; it is also a matter of immediate experience. For the traffic between our Old World and its antipodes, between Here and Beyond, travels along a two-way street. Gems, for example, come from the soul's visionary heaven; but they also lead the soul back to that heaven. Contemplating them, men find themselves (as the phrase goes) *transported* – carried away towards that Other Earth of the Platonic dialogue, the magical place where every pebble is a precious stone. And the same effects may be produced by artifacts of glass and metal, by tapers burning in the dark, by brilliantly coloured images and ornaments, by flowers, shells and feathers, by landscapes seen, as Shelley from the Euganean Hills saw Venice, in the transfiguring light of dawn or sunset.

Indeed, we may risk a generalization and say that whatever, in nature or in a work of art, resembles one of those intensely significant, inwardly glowing objects encountered at the mind's antipodes, is capable of inducing, if only in a partial and attenuated form, the visionary experience. At this point a hypnotist will remind us that, if he can be induced to stare intently at a shiny object, a patient may go into trance; and that if he goes into trance, or if he goes only into reverie, he may very well see visions within and a transfigured world without.

But how, precisely, and why does the view of a shiny object induce a trance or a state of reverie? Is it, as the

Victorians maintained, a simple matter of eye strain resulting in general nervous exhaustion? Or shall we explain the phenomenon in purely psychological terms – as concentration pushed to the point of mono-ideism and leading to dissociation?

But there is a third possibility. Shiny objects may remind our unconscious of what it enjoys at the mind's antipodes, and these obscure intimations of life in the Other World are so fascinating that we pay less attention to this world and so become capable of experiencing consciously something of that which, unconsciously, is always with us.

We see then that there are in nature certain scenes, certain classes of objects, certain materials, possessed of the power to transport the beholder's mind in the direction of its antipodes, out of the everyday Here and towards the Other World of Vision. Similarly, in the realm of art, we find certain works, even certain classes of works, in which the same transporting power is manifest. These vision-inducing works may be executed in vision-inducing materials, such as glass, metal, gems or gem-like pigments. In other cases their power is due to the fact that they render, in some peculiarly expressive way, some transporting scene or object.

The best vision-inducing art is produced by men and women who have themselves had the visionary experience; but it is also possible for any reasonably good artist, simply by following an approved recipe, to create works which shall have at least some transporting power.

Of all the vision-inducing arts that which depends most completely on its raw materials is, of course, the art of the goldsmith and jeweller. Polished metals and precious stones are so intrinsically transporting that even a Victorian, even an Art Nouveau jewel is a thing of power. And when to this natural magic of glinting metal and self-luminous stone is added the other magic of noble forms and colours artfully blended, we find ourselves in the presence of a genuine talisman.

Religious art has always and everywhere made use of these vision-inducing materials. The shrine of gold, the chryselephantine statue, the jewelled symbol or image, the glittering furniture of the altar – we find these things in contemporary Europe as in ancient Egypt, in India and China as among the Greeks, the Incas, the Aztecs.

The products of the goldsmith's art are intrinsically numinous. They have their place at the very heart of every Mystery, in every holy of holies. This sacred jewellery has always been associated with the light of lamps and candles. For Ezekiel, a gem was a stone of fire. Conversely, a flame is a living gem, endowed with all the transporting power that belongs to the precious stone and, to a lesser degree, to polished metal. This transporting power of flame increases in proportion to the depth and extent of the surrounding darkness. The most impressively numinous temples are caverns of twilight, in which a few tapers give life to the transporting, other-worldly treasures on the altar.

Glass is hardly less effective as an inducer of visions than are the natural gems. In certain respects, indeed, it is more effective, for the simple reason that there is more of it. Thanks to glass, a whole building – the Sainte-Chapelle, for example, the cathedrals of Chartres and Sens – could be turned into something magical and transporting. Thanks to glass, Paolo Uccello could design a circular jewel thirteen feet in diameter – his great window of the Resurrection, perhaps the most extraordinary single work of vision-inducing art ever produced.

For the men of the Middle Ages, it is evident, visionary experience was supremely valuable. So valuable, indeed, that they were ready to pay for it in hard-earned cash. In the twelfth century collecting-boxes were placed in the churches for the upkeep and installation of stained-glass windows. Suger, the Abbot of St Denis, tells us that they were always full.

But self-respecting artists cannot be expected to go on doing what their fathers have already done supremely well. In the fourteenth century colour gave place to grisaille, and windows ceased to be vision-inducing. When, in the later fifteenth century, colour came into fashion again, the glass painters felt the desire, and found themselves, at the same time, technically equipped, to imitate Renaissance painting in transparency. The results were often interesting; but they were not transporting.

Then came the Reformation. The Protestants disapproved of visionary experience and attributed a magical virtue to the printed word. In a church with clear windows the worshippers could read their Bibles and prayer books and were not tempted to escape from the sermon into the Other World. On the Catholic side the men of the Counter-Reformation found themselves in two minds. They thought visionary experience was a good thing, but they also believed in the supreme value of print.

In the new churches stained glass was rarely installed, and in many of the older churches it was wholly or partially replaced by clear glass. The unobscured light permitted the faithful to follow the service in their books, and at the same time to see the vision-inducing works created by the new generations of baroque sculptors and architects. These transporting works were executed in metal and polished stone. Wherever the worshipper turned, he found the glint of bronze, the rich radiance of coloured marble, the unearthly whiteness of statuary.

On the rare occasions when the Counter-Reformers made use of glass, it was as a surrogate for diamonds, not for rubies or sapphires. Faceted prisms entered religious art in the seventeenth century, and in Catholic churches they dangle to this day from innumerable chandeliers. (These charming and slightly ridiculous ornaments are among the very few vision-inducing devices permitted in Islam. Mosques have no images or reliquaries; but in the Near East, at any rate, their austerity is sometimes mitigated by the transporting glitter of rococo crystal.)

From glass, stained or cut, we pass to marble and the other stones that take a high polish and can be used in mass. The fascination exercised by such stones may be gauged by the amount of time and trouble spent in obtaining them. At Baalbek, for example, and, two or three hundred miles further inland, at Palmyra, we find among the ruins columns of pink granite from Aswan. These great monoliths were quarried in Upper Egypt, were floated in barges down the Nile, were towed across the Mediterranean to Byblos or Tripolis and from thence were hauled, by oxen, mules and men, uphill to Homs, and from Homs southward to Baalbek, or east, across the desert, to Palmyra.

What a labour of giants! And, from the utilitarian

point of view, how marvellously pointless! But in fact, of course, there was a point – a point that existed in a region beyond mere utility. Polished to a visionary glow, the rosy shafts proclaimed their manifest kinship with the Other World. At the cost of enormous efforts men had transported these stones from their quarry on the Tropic of Cancer; and now, by way of recompense, the stones were transporting their transporters halfway to the mind's visionary antipodes.

The question of utility and of the motives that lie beyond utility arises once more in relation to ceramics. Few things are more useful, more absolutely indispensable, than pots and plates and jugs. But at the same time few human beings concern themselves less with utility than do the collectors of porcelain and glazed earthenware. To say that these people have an appetite for beauty is not a sufficient explanation. The commonplace ugliness of the surroundings in which fine ceramics are so often displayed is proof enough that what their owners crave is not beauty in all its manifestations, but only a special kind of beauty – the beauty of curved reflections, of softly lustrous glazes, of sleek and smooth surfaces. In a word, the beauty that transports the beholder, because it reminds him, obscurely or explicitly, of the praeternatural lights and colours of the Other World. In the main the art of the potter has been a secular art – but a secular art which its innumerable devotees have treated with an almost idolatrous reverence. From time to time, however, this secular art has been placed at the service of religion. Glazed tiles have found their way into mosques and, here and there, into Christian churches. From China come shining ceramic images of gods and saints. In Italy Luca della

Robbia created a heaven of blue glaze, for his lustrous white madonnas and Christ children. Baked clay is cheaper than marble and, suitably treated, almost as transporting.

Plato and, during a later flowering of religious art, St Thomas Aquinas maintained that pure, bright colours were of the very essence of artistic beauty. A Matisse, in that case, could be intrinsically superior to a Goya or a Rembrandt. One has only to translate the philosophers' abstractions into concrete terms to see that this equation of beauty in general with bright, pure colours is absurd. But though untenable as it stands, the venerable doctrine is not altogether devoid of truth.

Bright, pure colours are characteristic of the Other World. Consequently works of art painted in bright, pure colours are capable, in suitable circumstances, of transporting the beholder's mind in the direction of its antipodes. Bright pure colours are of the essence, not of beauty in general, but only of a special kind of beauty, the visionary. Gothic churches and Greek temples, the statues of the thirteenth century after Christ and of the fifth century before Christ – all were brilliantly coloured.

For the Greeks and the men of the Middle Ages, this art of the merry-go-round and the wax-work show was evidently transporting. To us it seems deplorable. We prefer our Praxiteleses plain, our marble and out limestone *au naturel*. Why should our modern taste be so different, in this respect, from that of our ancestors? The reason, I presume, is that we have become too familiar with bright pure pigments to be greatly moved by them. We admire them, of course, when we see them in some grand or subtle composition; but in themselves and as such, they leave us un-transported.

Sentimental lovers of the past complain of the drabness of our age and contrast it unfavourably with the gay brilliance of earlier times. In actual fact, of course, there is a far greater profusion of colour in the modern than in the ancient world. Lapis lazuli and Tyrian purple were costly rarities; the rich velvets and brocades of princely wardrobes, the woven or painted hangings of mediaeval and early modern houses, were reserved for a privileged minority.

Even the great ones of the earth possessed very few of these vision-inducing treasures. As late as the seventeenth century, monarchs owned so little furniture that they had to travel from palace to palace with wagonloads of plate and bedspreads, of carpets and tapestries. For the great mass of the people there were only homespun and a few vegetable dyes; and, for interior decoration, there were at best the earth colours, at worst (and in most cases) 'the floor of plaster and the walls of dung.'

At the antipodes of every mind lay the Other World of praeternatural light and praeternatural colour, of ideal gems and visionary gold. But before every pair of eyes was only the dark squalor of the family hovel, the dust or mud of the village street, the dirty whites, the duns and goose-turd greens of ragged clothing. Hence a passionate, an almost desperate, thirst for bright, pure colours; and hence the overpowering effect produced by such colours whenever, in church or at court, they were displayed. Today the chemical industry turns out paints, inks and dyes in endless variety and enormous quantities. In our modern world there is enough bright colour to guarantee the production of billions of flags and comic strips, millions of stop signs and tail lights, fire engines and Coca-Cola containers by the hundred thousand, carpets, wallpapers and non-representational art by the square mile.

Familiarity breeds indifference. We have seen too much pure, bright colour at Woolworth's to find it intrinsically transporting. And here we may note that, by its amazing capacity to give us too much of the best things, modern technology has tended to devaluate the traditional vision-inducing materials. The illumination of a city, for example, was once a rare event, reserved for victories and national holidays, for the canonization of saints and the crowning of kings. Now it occurs nightly and celebrates the virtues of gin, cigarettes and toothpaste.

In London, fifty years ago, electric sky signs were a novelty and so rare that they shone out of the misty darkness 'like captain jewels in the carcanet.' Across the Thames, on the old Shot Tower, the gold and ruby letters were magically lovely – *une féerie.* Today the fairies are gone. Neon is everywhere and, being everywhere, has no effect upon us, except perhaps to make us pine nostalgically for primeval night.

Only in floodlighting do we recapture the unearthly significance which used, in the age of oil and wax, even in the age of gas and the carbon filament, to shine forth from practically any island of brightness in the boundless dark. Under the searchlights Notre-Dame de Paris and the Roman Forum are visionary objects, having power to transport the beholder's mind towards the Other World.[1]

Modern technology has had the same devaluating

[1] See Appendix III.

effect on glass and polished metal as it has had on fairy lamps and pure, bright colours. By John of Patmos and his contemporaries walls of glass were conceivable only in the New Jerusalem. Today they are a feature of every up-to-date office building and bungalow. And this glut of glass has been paralleled by a glut of chrome and nickel, of stainless steel and aluminium and a host of alloys old and new. Metal surfaces wink at us in the bathroom, shine from the kitchen sink, go ˘glittering across country in cars and trains.

Those rich convex reflections, which so fascinated Rembrandt that he never tired of rendering them in paint, are now the commonplaces of home and street and factory. The fine point of seldom pleasure has been blunted. What was once a needle of visionary delight has now become a piece of disregarded linoleum.

I have spoken so far only of vision-inducing materials and their psychological devaluation by modern technology. It is time now to consider the purely artistic devices, by means of which vision-inducing works have been created.

Light and colour tend to take on a praeternatural quality when seen in the midst of environing darkness. Fra Angelico's Crucifixion at the Louvre has a black background. So have the frescoes of the Passion painted by Andrea del Castagno for the nuns of Santa Apollonia at Florence. Hence the visionary intensity, the strange transporting power of these extraordinary works. In an entirely different artistic and psychological context the same device was often used by Goya in his etchings. Those flying men, that horse on a tightrope, the huge and ghastly incarnation of Fear – all of them stand out, as though floodlit, against a background of impenetrable night.

With the development of chiaroscuro, in the sixteenth and seventeenth centuries, night came out of the background and installed itself within the picture, which became the scene of a kind of Manichean struggle between Light and Darkness. At the time they were painted these works must have possessed a real transporting power. To us, who have seen altogether too much of this kind of thing, most of them seem merely theatrical. But a few still retain their magic. There is Caravaggio's *Entombment*, for example; there are a dozen magical paintings by Georges de Latour;[1] there are all those visionary Rembrandts where the lights have the intensity and significance of light at the mind's antipodes, where the darks are full of rich potentialities waiting their turn to become actual, to make themselves glowingly present to our consciousness.

In most cases the ostensible subject-matter of Rembrandt's pictures is taken from real life or the Bible – a boy at his lessons or Bathsheba bathing; a woman wading in a pond or Christ before His judges. Occasionally, however, these messages from the Other World are transmitted by means of a subject drawn, not from real life or history, but from the realm of archetypal symbols. There hangs in the Louvre a *Méditation du Philosophe*, whose symbolical subject-matter is nothing more or less than the human mind, with its teeming darknesses, its moments of intellectual and visionary illumination, its mysterious stairways winding downwards and upwards into the unknown. The meditating philosopher sits there in his island of inner illumination; and

[1] See Appendix IV.

at the opposite end of the symbolic chamber, in another, rosier island, an old woman crouches before the hearth. The firelight touches and transfigures her face, and we see, concretely illustrated, the impossible paradox and supreme truth – that perception is (or at least can be, ought to be) the same as Revelation, that Reality shines out of every appearance, that the One is totally, infinitely present in all particulars.

Along with the praeternatural lights and colours, the gems and the ever-changing patterns, visitors to the mind's antipodes discover a world of sublimely beautiful landscapes, of living architecture and of heroic figures. The transporting power of many works of art is attributable to the fact that their creators have painted scenes, persons and objects which remind the beholder of what, consciously or unconsciously, he knows about the Other World at the back of his mind.

Let us begin with the human or, rather, the more than human inhabitants of these far-off regions. Blake called them the Cherubim. And in effect that is what, no doubt, they are—the psychological originals of those beings who, in the theology of every religion, serve as intermediaries between man and the Clear Light. The more than human personages of visionary experience never 'do anything.' (Similarly the blessed never 'do anything' in heaven.) They are content merely to exist.

Under many names and attired in an endless variety of costumes, these heroic figures of man's visionary experience have appeared in the religious art of every culture. Sometimes they are shown at rest, sometimes in historical or mythological action. But action, as we have seen, does not come naturally to the inhabitants of the mind's antipodes. To be busy is the law of *our* being.

The law of *theirs* is to do nothing. When we force these serene strangers to play a part in one of our all too human dramas, we are being false to visionary truth. That is why the most transporting (though not necessarily the most beautiful) representation of 'the Cherubim' are those which show them as they are in their native habitat – doing nothing in particular.

And that accounts for the overwhelming, the more than merely aesthetic, impression made upon the beholder by the great static masterpieces of religious art. The sculptured figures of Egyptian gods and godkings, the Madonnas and Pantocrators of the Byzantine mosaics, the Bodhisattvas and Lohans of China, the seated Buddhas of Khmer, the steles and statues of Copan, the wooden idols of tropical Africa – these have one characteristic in common: a profound stillness. And it is precisely this which gives them their numinous quality, their power to transport the beholder out of the Old World of his everyday experience, far away, towards the visionary antipodes of the human psyche.

There is, of course, nothing intrinsically excellent about static art. Static or dynamic, a bad piece of work is always a bad piece of work. All I mean to imply is that, other things being equal, a heroic figure at rest has a greater transporting power than one which is shown in action.

The Cherubim live in Paradise and the New Jerusalem – in other words, among prodigious buildings set in rich, bright gardens with distant prospects of plain and mountain, of rivers and the sea. This is a matter of immediate experience, a psychological fact which has been recorded in folklore and the religious literature of every age and country. It has not, however, been recorded in pictorial art.

Reviewing the succession of human cultures, we find that landscape painting is either non-existent, or rudimentary, or of very recent development. In Europe a full-blown art of landscape painting has existed for only four or five centuries, in China for not more than a thousand years, in India, for all practical purposes, never.

This is a curious fact that demands an explanation. Why should landscapes have found their way into the visionary literature of a given epoch and a given culture, but not into the painting? Posed in this way, the question provides its own best answer. People may be content with the merely verbal expression of this aspect of their visionary experience and feel no need for its translation into pictorial terms.

That this often happens in the case of individuals is certain. Blake, for example, saw visionary landscapes, 'articulated beyond all that the mortal and perishing nature can produce' and 'infinitely more perfect and minutely organized than anything seen by the mortal eye.' Here is the description of such a visionary landscape, which Blake gave at one of Mrs Aders' evening parties: 'The other evening, taking a walk, I came to a meadow and at the further corner of it I saw a fold of lambs. Coming nearer, the ground blushed with flowers, and the wattled cote and its woolly tenants were of an exquisite pastoral beauty. But I looked again, and it proved to be no living flock, but beautiful sculpture.'

Rendered in pigments, this vision would look, I suppose, like some impossibly beautiful blending of one of Constable's freshest oil sketches with an animal painting in the magically realistic style of Zurbaran's haloed lamb now in the San Diego Museum. But Blake never produced anything remotely resembling such a picture. He was content to talk and write about his landscape visions, and to concentrate in his painting upon 'the Cherubim.'

What is true of an individual artist may be true of a whole school. There are plenty of things which men experience, but do not choose to express; or they may try to express what they have experienced, but in only one of their arts. In yet other cases they will express themselves in ways having no immediately recognizable affinity to the original experience. In this last context Dr A. K. Coomaraswamy has some interesting things to say about the mystical art of the Far East – the art where 'denotation and connotation cannot be divided' and 'no distinction is felt between what a thing "is" and what it "signifies."'

The supreme example of such mystical art is the Zen-inspired landscape painting, which arose in China during the Sung period and came to new birth in Japan four centuries later. India and the Near East have no mystical landscape painting; but they have its equivalents – 'Vaisnava painting, poetry and music in India, where the theme is sexual love; and Sufi poetry and music in Persia, devoted to praises of intoxication.'[1]

'Bed,' as the Italian proverb succinctly puts it, 'is the poor man's opera.' Analogously, sex is the Hindu's Sung; wine, the Persian's Impressionism. The reason being, of course, that the experiences of sexual union and intoxication partake of that essential otherness characteristic of all vision, including that of landscapes.

If, at any time, men have found satisfaction in a certain kind of activity, it is to be presumed that, at periods when this satisfying activity was not mani-

[1] A. K. Coomaraswamy, *The Transformation of Nature in Art*, p. 40.

fested, there must have been some kind of equivalent for it. In the Middle Ages, for example, men were pre-occupied in an obsessive, an almost maniacal way with words and symbols. Everything in nature was instantly recognized as the concrete illustration of some notion formulated in one of the books or legends currently regarded as sacred.

And yet, at other periods of history men have found a deep satisfaction in recognizing the autonomous otherness of nature, including many aspects of human nature. The experience of this otherness was expressed in terms of art, religion or science. What were the mediaeval equivalents of Constable and ecology, of bird watching and Eleusis, of microscopy and the rites of Dionysos and the Japanese Haiku? They were to be found, I suspect, in Saturnalian orgies at one end of the scale and in mystical experience at the other. Shrove-tides, May Days, Carnivals – these permitted a direct experience of the animal otherness underlying personal and social identity. Infused contemplation revealed the yet otherer otherness of the divine Not-Self. And somewhere between the two extremes were the experiences of the visionaries and the vision-inducing arts, by means of which it was sought to recapture and re-create those experiences – the art of the jeweller, of the maker of stained glass, of the weaver of tapestries, of the painter, poet and musician.

In spite of a Natural History that was nothing but a set of drearily moralistic symbols, in the teeth of a theology which, instead of regarding words as the signs of things, treated things and events as the signs of biblical or Aristotelian words, our ancestors remained relatively sane. And they achieved this feat by perio-dically escaping from the stifling prison of their bumptiously rationalistic philosophy, their anthropomorphic, authoritarian and non-experimental science, their all too articulate religion, into non-verbal, other than human worlds inhabited by their instincts, by the visionary fauna of their mind's antipodes and, beyond and yet within all the rest, by the indwelling Spirit.

From this wide-ranging but necessary digression, let us return to the particular case from which we set out. Landscapes, as we have seen, are a regular feature of the visionary experience. Descriptions of visionary landscapes occur in the ancient literature of folklore and religion; but paintings of landscapes do not make their appearance until comparatively recent times. To what has been said, by way of explanation about psychological equivalents, I will add a few brief notes on the nature of landscape paintings as a vision-inducing art.

Let us begin by asking a question. What landscapes – or, more generally, what representations of natural objects – are most transporting, most intrinsically vision-inducing? In the light of my own experiences and of what I have heard other people say about their reactions to works of art, I will risk an answer. Other things being equal (for nothing can make up for lack of talent), the most transporting landscapes are, first, those which represent natural objects a very long way off, and, second, those which represent them at close range.

Distance lends enchantment to the view; but so does propinquity. A Sung painting of far away mountains, clouds and torrents is transporting; but so are the close-ups of tropical leaves in the Douanier Rousseau's jungles. When I look at the Sung landscape, I am reminded (or one of my not-I's is reminded) of the crags, the boundless expanses of plain, the luminous skies and seas of the mind's antipodes. And those disappearances into mist and cloud, those sudden emergences of some strange, intensely definite form, a weathered rock, for example, an ancient pine tree twisted by years of struggle with the wind – these too, are transporting. For they remind me, consciously or unconsciously, of the Other World's essential alienness and unaccountability.

It is the same with the close-up. I look at those leaves with their architecture of veins, their stripes and mottlings, I peer into the depths of interlacing greenery, and something in me is reminded of those living patterns, so characteristic of the visionary world, of those endless births and proliferations of geometrical forms that turn into objects, of things that are forever being transmuted into other things.

This painted close-up of a jungle is what, on one of its aspects, the Other World is like, and so it transports me, it makes me see with eyes that transfigure a work of art into something else, something beyond art.

I remember – very vividly, though it took place many years ago – a conversation with Roger Fry. We were talking about Monet's 'Water Lilies.' They had no right, Roger kept insisting, to be so shockingly unorganized, so totally without a proper compositional skeleton. They were all wrong, artistically speaking. And yet, he had to admit, and yet. ... And yet, as I should now say, they were transporting. An artist of astounding virtuosity had chosen to paint a close-up of natural objects seen in their own context and without reference to merely human notions of what's what, or what ought to be what. Man, we like to say, is the measure of all things. For Monet, on this occasion, water lilies were the measure of water lilies; and so he painted them.

The same non-human point of view must be adopted by any artist who tries to render the distant scene. How tiny, in the Chinese painting, are the travellers who make their way along the valley! How frail the bamboo hut on the slope above them! And all the rest of the vast landscape is emptiness and silence. This revelation of the wilderness, living its own life according to the laws of its own being, transports the mind towards its antipodes; for primeval Nature bears a strange resemblance to that inner world where no account is taken of our personal wishes or even of the enduring concerns of man in general.

Only the middle distance and what may be called the remoter foreground are strictly human. When we look very near or very far, man either vanishes altogether or loses his primacy. The astronomer looks even further afield than the Sung painter and sees even less of human life. At the other end of the scale the physicist, the chemist, the physiologist pursue the close-up – the cellular close-up, the molecular, the atomic and sub-atomic. Of that which, at twenty feet, even at arm's length, looked and sounded like a human being no trace remains.

Something analogous happens to the myopic artist and the happy lover. In the nuptial embrace personality is melted down; the individual (it is the recurrent theme of Lawrence's poems and novels) ceases to be himself and becomes a part of the vast impersonal universe.

And so it is with the artist who chooses to use his eyes at the near point. In his work humanity loses its importance, even disappears completely. Instead of men and women playing their fantastic tricks before high heaven, we are asked to consider the lilies, to meditate on the unearthly beauty of 'mere things,' when isolated from their utilitarian context and rendered as they are, in and for themselves. Alternatively (or, at an earlier stage of artistic development, exclusively), the non-human world of the near-point is rendered in patterns. These patterns are abstracted for the most part from leaves and flowers – the rose, the lotus, the acanthus, palm, papyrus – and are elaborated, with recurrences and variations, into something transportingly reminiscent of the living geometries of the Other World.

Freer and more realistic treatments of Nature at the near-point make their appearance at a relatively recent date – but far earlier than those treatments of the distant scene, to which alone (and mistakenly) we give the name of landscape painting. Rome, for example, had its close-up landscapes. The fresco of a garden, which once adorned a room in Livia's villa, is a magnificent example of this form of art.

For theological reasons, Islam had to be content, for the most part, with 'arabesques' – luxuriant and (as in visions) continually varying patterns, based upon natural objects seen at the near-point. But even in Islam the genuine close-up landscape was not unknown. Nothing can exceed in beauty and in vision-inducing power the mosaics of gardens and buildings in the great Omayyad mosque at Damascus.

In mediaeval Europe, despite the prevailing mania for turning every datum into a concept, every immediate experience into a mere symbol of something in a book, realistic close-ups of foliage and flowers were fairly common. We find them carved on the capitals of

Gothic pillars, as in the Chapter House of Southwell Minster. We find them in paintings of the chase – paintings whose subject was that ever present fact of mediaeval life, the forest, seen as the hunter or the strayed traveller sees it, in all its bewildering intricacy of leafy detail.

The frescoes in the papal palace at Avignon are almost the sole survivors of what, even in the time of Chaucer, was a widely practised form of secular art. A century later this art of the forest close-up came to its self-conscious perfection in such magnificent and magical works as Pisanello's *St Hubert* and Paolo Uccello's *Hunt in a Wood*, now in the Ashmolean Museum at Oxford. Closely related to the wall paintings of forest close-ups were the tapestries, with which the rich men of northern Europe adorned their houses. The best of these are vision-inducing works of the highest order. In their own way they are as heavenly, as powerfully reminiscent of what goes on at the mind's antipodes, as are the great masterpieces of landscape painting at the furthest point – Sung mountains in their enormous solitude, Ming rivers interminably lovely, the blue sub-Alpine world of Titian's distances, the England of Constable; the Italies of Turner and Corot; the Provences of Cézanne and Van Gogh; the Île de France of Sisley and the Île de France of Vuillard.

Vuillard, incidentally, was a supreme master both of the transporting close-up and of the transporting distant view. His bourgeois interiors are masterpieces of vision-inducing art, compared with which the works of such conscious and so to say professional visionaries as Blake and Odilon Redon seem feeble in the extreme. In Vuillard's interiors every detail however trivial, however hideous even – the pattern of the late Victorian wall-

97

paper, the Art Nouveau bibelot, the Brussels carpet – is seen and rendered as a living jewel; and all these jewels are harmoniously combined into a whole which is a jewel of a yet higher order of visionary intensity. And when the upper middle-class inhabitants of Vuillard's New Jerusalem go for a walk, they find themselves not, as they had supposed, in the department of Seine et Oise, but in the Garden of Eden, in an Other World which is yet essentially the same as this world, but transfigured and therefore transporting.[1]

I have spoken so far only of the blissful visionary experience and of its interpretation in terms of theology, its translation into art. But visionary experience is not always blissful. It is sometimes terrible. There is hell as well as heaven.

Like heaven, the visionary hell has its praeternatural light and its praeternatural significance. But the significance is intrinsically appalling and the light is 'the smoky light' of the *Tibetan Book of the Dead*, the 'darkness visible' of Milton. In the *Journal d'une Schizophrène*,[2] the autobiographical record of a young girl's passage through madness, the world of the schizophrenic is called *le Pays d'Éclairement* – 'the country of lit-upness.' It is a name which a mystic might have used to denote his heaven.

But for poor Renée, the schizophrenic, the illumination is infernal – an intense electric glare without a shadow, ubiquitous and implacable. Everything that, for healthy visionaries, is a source of bliss, brings to Renée only fear and a nightmarish sense of unreality. The summer sunshine is malignant; the gleam of

---

[1] See Appendix V.
[2] *Journal d'une Schizophrène*, by M. A. Sèchehaye. Paris, 1950.

polished surfaces is suggestive, not of gems, but of machinery and enamelled tin; the intensity of existence which animates every object, when seen at close range and out of its utilitarian context, is felt as a menace.

And then there is the horror of infinity. For the healthy visionary, the perception of the infinite in a finite particular is a revelation of divine immanence; for Renée, it was a revelation of what she calls 'the System,' the vast cosmic mechanism which exists only to grind out guilt and punishment, solitude and un-reality.[1]

Sanity is a matter of degree, and there are plenty of visionaries who see the world as Renée saw it, but contrive, none the less, to live outside the asylum. For them, as for the positive visionary, the universe is trans-figured – but for the worse. Everything in it, from the stars in the sky to the dust under their feet, is unspeak-ably sinister or disgusting; every event is charged with a hateful significance; every object manifests the pre-sence of an Indwelling Horror, infinite, all-powerful, eternal.

This negatively transfigured world has found its way, from time to time, into literature and the arts. It writhed and threatened in Van Gogh's later land-scapes; it was the setting and the theme of all Kafka's stories; it was Géricault's spiritual home;[2] it was inhabited by Goya during the years of his deafness and solitude; it was glimpsed by Browning when he wrote *Childe Roland*; it had its place, over against the theo-phanies, in the novels of Charles Williams.

The negative visionary experience is often accom-panied by bodily sensations of a very special and char-acteristic kind. Blissful visions are generally associated

[1] See Appendix VI. [2] See Appendix VII.

99

with a sense of separation from the body, a feeling of deindividualization. (It is, no doubt, this feeling of deindividualization which makes it possible for the Indians who practise the peyote cult to use the drug not merely as a short cut to the visionary world, but also as an instrument for creating a loving solidarity within the participating group.) When the visionary experience is terrible and the world is transfigured for the worse, individualization is intensified and the negative visionary finds himself associated with a body that seems to grow progressively more dense, more tightly packed, until he finds himself at last reduced to being the agonized consciousness of an inspissated lump of matter, no bigger than a stone that can be held between the hands.

It is worth remarking, that many of the punishments described in the various accounts of hell are punishments of pressure and constriction. Dante's sinners are buried in mud, shut up in the trunks of trees, frozen solid in blocks of ice, crushed beneath stones. The *Inferno* is psychologically true. Many of its pains are experienced by schizophrenics, and by those who have taken mescalin or lysergic acid under unfavourable conditions.[1]

What is the nature of these unfavourable conditions? How and why is heaven turned into hell? In certain cases the negative visionary experience is the result of predominantly physical causes. Mescalin tends, after ingestion, to accumulate in the liver. If the liver is diseased, the associated mind may find itself in hell. But what is more important for our present purposes is the fact that negative visionary experience may be

[1] See Appendix VIII.

induced by purely psychological means. Fear and anger bar the way to the heavenly Other World and plunge the mescalin taker into hell.

And what is true of the mescalin taker is also true of the person who sees visions spontaneously or under hypnosis. Upon this psychological foundation has been reared the theological doctrine of saving faith – a doctrine to be met with in all the great religious traditions of the world. Eschatologists have always found it difficult to reconcile their rationality and their morality with the brute facts of psychological experience. As rationalists and moralists, they feel that good behaviour should be rewarded and that the virtuous deserve to go to heaven. But as psychologists they know that virtue is not the sole or sufficient condition of blissful visionary experience. They know that works alone are powerless and that it is faith, or loving confidence, which guarantees that visionary experience shall be blissful.

Negative emotions – the fear which is the absence of confidence, the hatred, anger or malice which exclude love – are the guarantee that visionary experience, if and when it comes, shall be appalling. The Pharisee is a virtuous man; but his virtue is of the kind which is compatible with negative emotion. His visionary experiences are therefore likely to be infernal rather than blissful.

The nature of the mind is such that the sinner who repents and makes an act of faith in a higher power is more likely to have a blissful visionary experience than is the self-satisfied pillar of society with his righteous indignations, his anxiety about possessions and pretensions, his ingrained habits of blaming, despising and condemning. Hence the enormous importance attached, in all the great religious traditions, to the state of mind at the moment of death.

Visionary experience is not the same as mystical experience. Mystical experience is beyond the realm of opposites. Visionary experience is still within that realm. Heaven entails hell, and 'going to heaven' is no more liberation than is the descent into horror. Heaven is merely a vantage point from which the divine Ground can be more clearly seen than on the level of ordinary individualized existence.

If consciousness survives bodily death, it survives, presumably, on every mental level – on the level of mystical experience, on the level of blissful visionary experience, on the level of infernal visionary experience, and on the level of everyday individual existence.

In life, even the blissful visionary experience tends to change its sign if it persists too long. Many schizophrenics have their times of heavenly happiness; but the fact that (unlike the mescalin taker) they do not know when, if ever, they will be permitted to return to the reassuring banality of everyday experience causes even heaven to seem appalling. But for those who, for whatever reason, are appalled, heaven turns into hell, bliss into horror, the Clear Light into the hateful glare of the land of lit-upness.

Something of the same kind may happen in the posthumous state. After having had a glimpse of the unbearable splendour of ultimate Reality, and after having shuttled back and forth between heaven and hell, most souls find it possible to retreat into that more reassuring region of the mind, where they can use their own and other people's wishes, memories and fancies to construct a world very like that in which they lived . on earth.

Of those who die an infinitesimal minority are capable of immediate union with the divine Ground, a few are capable of supporting the visionary bliss of heaven, a few find themselves in the visionary horrors of hell and are unable to escape; the great majority end up in the kind of world described by Swedenborg and the mediums. From this world it is doubtless possible to pass, when the necessary conditions have been fulfilled, to worlds of visionary bliss or the final enlightenment.

My own guess is that modern spiritualism and ancient tradition are both correct. There *is* a posthumous state of the kind described in Sir Oliver Lodge's book, *Raymond*; but there is also a heaven of blissful visionary experience; there is also a hell of the same kind of appalling visionary experience as is suffered here by schizophrenics and some of those who take mescalin and there is also an experience, beyond time, of union with the divine Ground.

Appendix I

Two other, less effective aids to visionary experience deserve mention – carbon dioxide and the stroboscopic lamp. A mixture (completely non-toxic) of seven parts of oxygen and three of carbon dioxide produces, in those who inhale it, certain physical and psychological changes, which have been exhaustively described by Meduna. Among these changes the most important, in our present context, is a marked enhancement of the ability to 'see things,' when the eyes are closed. In some cases only swirls of patterned colour are seen. In others there may be vivid recalls of past experiences. (Hence the value of CO_2 as a therapeutic agent.) In yet other cases carbon dioxide transports the subject to the Other World at the antipodes of his everyday consciousness, and he enjoys very briefly visionary experiences entirely unconnected with his own personal history or with the problems of the human race in general.

In the light of these facts it becomes easy to understand the rationale of yogic breathing exercises. Practised systematically, these exercises result, after a time, in prolonged suspensions of breath. Long suspensions of breath lead to a high concentration of carbon dioxide in the lungs and blood, and this increase in the concentration of CO_2 lowers the efficiency of the brain as a reducing valve and permits the entry into consciousness of experiences, visionary or mystical, from 'out there.'

Prolonged and continuous shouting or singing may produce similar, but less strongly marked, results.

Unless they are highly trained, singers tend to breathe out more than they breathe in. Consequently the concentration of carbon dioxide in the alveolar air and the blood is increased and, the efficiency of the cerebral reducing valve being lowered, visionary experience becomes possible. Hence the interminable 'vain repetitions' of magic and religion. The chanting of the *curandero*, the medicine-man, the shaman; the endless psalm-singing and sutra-intoning of Christian and Buddhist monks; the shouting and howling, hour after hour, of revivalists – under all the diversities of theological belief and aesthetic convention, the psycho-chemico-physiological intention remains constant. To increase the concentration of CO_2 in the lungs and blood and so to lower the efficiency of the cerebral reducing valve, until it will admit biologically useless material from Mind-at-Large – this, though the shouters, singers and mutterers did not know it, has been at all times the real purpose and point of magic spells, of mantrams, litanies, psalms and sutras. 'The heart,' said Pascal, 'has its reasons.' Still more cogent and much harder to unravel are the reasons of the lungs, the blood and the enzymes, of neurones and synapses. The way to the superconscious is through the subconscious, and the way, or at least one of the ways, to the subconscious is through the chemistry of individual cells.

With the stroboscopic lamp we descend from chemistry to the still more elementary realm of physics. Its rhythmically flashing light seems to act directly, through the optic nerves, on the electrical manifestations of the brain's activity. (For this reason there is always a slight danger involved in the use of the stroboscopic lamp. Some persons suffer from *petit mal* without being made aware of the fact by any clear-cut and unmistakable symptoms. Exposed to a stroboscopic lamp, such persons may go into a full-blown epileptic fit. The risk is not very great; but it must always be recognized. One case in eighty may turn out badly.

To sit, with eyes closed, in front of a stroboscopic lamp is a very curious and fascinating experience. No sooner is the lamp turned on than the most brilliantly coloured patterns make themselves visible. These patterns are not static, but change incessantly. Their prevailing colour is a function of the stroboscope's rate of discharge. When the lamp is flashing at any speed between ten to fourteen or fifteen times a second, the patterns are prevailingly orange and red. Green and blue make their appearance when the rate exceeds fifteen flashes a second. After eighteen or nineteen, the patterns become white and grey. Precisely why we should see such patterns under the stroboscope is not known. The most obvious explanation would be in terms of the interference of two or more rhythms – the rhythm of the lamp and the various rhythms of the brain's electrical activity. Such interferences may be translated by the visual centre and optic nerves into something, of which the mind becomes conscious as a coloured, moving pattern. Far more difficult to explain is the fact, independently observed by several experimenters, that the stroboscope tends to enrich and intensify the visions induced by mescalin or lysergic acid. Here, for example, is a case communicated to me by a medical friend. He had taken lysergic acid and was seeing, with his eyes shut, only coloured, moving patterns. Then he sat down in front of a stroboscope. The lamp was turned on and, immediately, abstract geometry was transformed into what my friend described as 'Japanese landscapes' of surpassing beauty.

But how on earth can the interference of two rhythms produce an arrangement of electrical impulses interpretable as a living, self-modulating Japanese landscape unlike anything the subject has ever seen, suffused with praeternatural light and colour, and charged with praeternatural significance?

This mystery is merely a particular case of a larger, more comprehensive mystery – the nature of the relations between visionary experience and events on the cellular, chemical and electrical levels. By touching certain areas of the brain with a very fine electrode, Penfield has been able to induce the recall of a long chain of memories relating to some past experience. This recall is not merely accurate on every perceptual detail; it is also accompanied by all the emotions which were aroused by the events when they originally occurred. The patient, who is under a local anaesthetic, finds himself simultaneously in two times and places – in the operating room, now, and in his childhood home, hundreds of miles away and thousands of days in the past. Is there, one wonders, some area in the brain from which the probing electrode could elicit Blake's Cherubim, or Weir Mitchell's self-transforming Gothic tower encrusted with living gems, or my friend's unspeakably lovely Japanese landscapes? And if, as I myself believe, visionary experiences enter our consciousness from somewhere 'out there' in the infinity of Mind-at-Large, what sort of an *ad hoc* neurological pattern is created for them by the receiving and transmitting brain? And what happens to this *ad hoc* pattern, when the vision is over? Why do all visionaries insist on the impossibility of recalling, in anything even faintly resembling its original form and intensity, their transfiguring experiences? How many questions – and, as yet, how few answers!

Appendix II

In the Western world visionaries and mystics are a good deal less common than they used to be. There are two principal reasons for this state of affairs – a philosophical reason and a chemical reason. In the currently fashionable picture of the universe there is no place for valid transcendental experience. Consequently those who have had what they regard as valid transcendental experiences are looked upon with suspicion, as being either lunatics or swindlers. To be a mystic or a visionary is no longer creditable.

But it is not only our mental climate that is unfavourable to the visionary and the mystic; it is also our chemical environment – an environment profoundly different from that in which our forefathers passed their lives.

The brain is chemically controlled, and experience has shown that it can be made permeable to the (biologically speaking) superfluous aspects of Mind-at-Large by modifying the (biologically speaking) normal chemistry of the body.

For almost half of every year our ancestors ate no fruit, no green vegetables and (since it was impossible for them to feed more than a few oxen, cows, swine and poultry during the winter months) very little butter or fresh meat, and very few eggs. By the beginning of each successive spring, most of them were suffering, mildly or acutely, from scurvy, due to lack of vitamin C, and pellagra, caused by a shortage in their diet of the B complex. The distressing physical symptoms of these diseases are associated with no less distressing psychological symptoms.[1]

The nervous system is more vulnerable than the other tissues of the body; consequently vitamin deficiencies tend to affect the state of mind before they affect, at least in any very obvious way, the skin, bones, mucous membranes, muscles and viscera. The first result of an inadequate diet is a lowering of the efficiency of the brain as an instrument for biological survival. The undernourished person tends to be afflicted by anxiety, depression, hypochondria and feelings of anxiety. He is also liable to see visions; for when the cerebral reducing valve has its efficiency reduced, much (biologically speaking) useless material flows into consciousness from 'out there,' in Mind-at-Large.

Much of what the earlier visionaries experienced was terrifying. To use the language of Christian theology, the Devil revealed himself in their visions and ecstasies a good deal more frequently than did God. In an age. when vitamins were deficient and a belief in Satan universal, this was not surprising. The mental distress, associated with even mild cases of pellagra and scurvy, was deepened by fears of damnation and a conviction that the powers of evil were omnipresent. This distress was apt to tinge with its own dark colouring the visionary material, admitted to consciousness through a cerebral valve whose efficiency had been impaired by underfeeding. But in spite of their preoccupations with eternal punishment and in spite of their deficiency disease, spiritually minded ascetics often saw heaven

[1] See *The Biology of Human Starvation*, by A. Keys (University of Minnesota Press 1950); also the recent (1955) reports of the work on the role of vitamin deficiencies in mental disease carried out by Dr George Watson and his associates in Southern California.

and might even be aware, occasionally, of that divinely impartial One, in which the polar opposites are reconciled. For a glimpse of beatitude, for a foretaste of unitive knowledge, no price seemed too high. Mortification of the body may produce a host of undesirable mental symptoms; but it may also open a door into a transcendental world of Being, Knowledge and Bliss. That is why, in spite of its obvious disadvantages, almost all aspirants to the spiritual life have, in the past, undertaken regular courses of bodily mortification.

So far as vitamins were concerned, every mediaeval winter was a long involuntary fast, and this involuntary fast was followed, during Lent, by forty days of voluntary abstinence. Holy Week found the faithful marvellously well prepared, so far as their body chemistry was concerned, for its tremendous incitements to grief and joy, for seasonable remorse of conscience and a self-transcending identification with the risen Christ. At this season of the highest religious excitement and the lowest vitamin intake, ecstasies and visions were almost a commonplace. It was only to be expected.

For cloistered contemplatives, there were several Lents in every year. And even between fasts their diet was meagre in the extreme. Hence those agonies of depression and scrupulosity described by so many spiritual writers; hence their frightful temptations to despair and self-slaughter. But hence too those 'gratuitous graces,' in the form of heavenly visions and locutions, of prophetic insights, of telepathic 'discernments of spirits.' And hence, finally, their 'infused contemplation,' their 'obscure knowledge' of the One in all.

Fasting was not the only form of physical mortification resorted to by the earlier aspirants to spirituality.

Most of them regularly used upon themselves the whip of knotted leather or even of iron wire. These beatings were the equivalent of fairly extensive surgery without anaesthetics, and their effects on the body chemistry of the penitent were considerable. Large quantities of histamine and adrenalin were released while the whip was actually being plied; and when the resulting wounds began to fester (as wounds practically always did before the age of soap), various toxic substances, produced by the decomposition of protein, found their way into the bloodstream. But histamine produces shock, and shock affects the mind no less profoundly than the body. Moreover, large quantities of adrenalin may cause hallucinations, and some of the products of its decomposition are known to induce symptoms resembling those of schizophrenia. As for toxins from wounds – these upset the enzyme systems regulating the brain, and lower its efficiency as an instrument for getting on in a world where the biologically fittest survive. This may explain why the Curé d'Ars used to say that, in the days when he was free to flagellate himself without mercy, God would refuse him nothing. In other words, when remorse, self-loathing and the fear of hell release adrenalin, when self-inflicted surgery releases adrenalin and histamine and when infected wounds release decomposed protein into the blood, the efficiency of the cerebral reducing valve is lowered and unfamiliar aspects of Mind-at-Large (including psi phenomena, visions and, if he is philosophically and ethically prepared for it, mystical experiences) will flow into the ascetic's consciousness.

Lent, as we have seen, followed a long period of involuntary fasting. Analogously, the effects of self-flagellation were supplemented, in earlier times, by much involuntary absorption of decomposed protein. Dentistry was non-existent, surgeons were executioners and there were no safe antiseptics. Most people, therefore, must have lived out their lives with focal infections; and focal infections, though out of fashion as the cause of *all* the ills that flesh is heir to, can certainly lower the efficiency of the cerebral reducing valve.

And the moral of all this is – what? Exponents of a Nothing-But philosophy will answer that, since changes in body chemistry can create the conditions favourable to visionary and mystical experience, visionary and mystical experience cannot be what they claim to be – what, for those who have had them, they self-evidently are. But this, of course, is a *non sequitur*.

A similar conclusion will be reached by those whose philosophy is unduly 'spiritual.' God, they will insist, is a spirit and is to be worshipped in spirit. Therefore an experience which is chemically conditioned cannot be an experience of the divine. But, in one way or another, *all* our experiences are chemically conditioned, and if we imagine that some of them are purely 'spiritual,' purely 'intellectual,' purely 'aesthetic,' it is merely because we have never troubled to investigate the internal chemical environment at the moment of their occurrence. Furthermore, it is a matter of historical record that most contemplatives worked systematically to modify their body chemistry, with a view to creating the internal conditions favourable to spiritual insight. When they were not starving themselves into low blood sugar and a vitamin deficiency, or beating themselves into intoxication by histamine, adrenalin and decomposed protein, they were cultivating insomnia and praying for long periods in uncomfortable positions, in order to create the psycho-physical symptoms of stress. In the intervals they sang interminable psalms, thus increasing the amount of carbon dioxide in the lungs and the blood-stream, or, if they were Orientals, they did breathing exercises to accomplish the same purpose. Today we know how to lower the efficiency of the cerebral reducing valve by direct chemical action, and without the risk of inflicting serious damage on the psycho-physical organism. For an aspiring mystic to revert, in the present state of knowledge, to prolonged fasting and violent self-flagellation would be as senseless as it would be for an aspiring cook to behave like Charles Lamb's Chinaman, who burned down the house in order to roast a pig. Knowing as he does (or at least as he can know, if he so desires) what are the chemical conditions of transcendental experience, the aspiring mystic should turn for technical help to the specialists – in pharmacology, in biochemistry, in physiology and neurology, in psychology and psychiatry and parapsychology. And on their part, of course, the specialists (if any of them aspire to be genuine men of science and complete human beings) should turn, out of their respective pigeon-holes, to the artist, the sibyl, the visionary, the mystic – all those, in a word, who have had experience of the Other World and who know, in their different ways, what to do with that experience.

Appendix III

Vision-like effects and vision-inducing devices have played a greater part in popular entertainment than in the fine arts. Fireworks, pageantry, theatrical spectacle – these are essentially visionary arts. Unfortunately they are also ephemeral arts, whose earlier master-pieces are known to us only by report. Nothing remains of all the Roman triumphs, the mediaeval tournaments, the Jacobean masques, the long succession of state entries and coronations, of royal marriages and solemn decapitations, of canonizations and the funerals of Popes. The best that can be hoped for such magnificences is that they may 'live in Settle's numbers one day more.'

An interesting feature of these popular visionary arts is their close dependence upon contemporary technology. Fireworks, for example, were once no more than bonfires (and to this day, I may add, a good bonfire on a dark night remains one of the most magical and transporting of spectacles. Looking at it, one can understand the mentality of the Mexican peasant, who sets out to burn an acre of woodland in order to plant his maize, but is delighted when, by a happy accident, a square mile or two goes up in bright, apocalyptic flame). True pyrotechny began (in Europe at least, if not in China) with the use of combustibles in sieges and naval battles. From war it passed, in due course, to entertainment. Imperial Rome had its firework displays, some of which, even in its decline, were elaborate in the extreme. Here is Claudian's description of the show put on by Manlius Theodorus in A.D. 399.

Mobile ponderibus descendat pegma reductis
inque chori speciem spargentes ardua flammas
scaena rotet varios, et fingat Mulciber orbis
per tabulas impune vagos pictaeque citato
ludant igne trabes, et non permissa morari
fida per innocuas errent incendia turres.

'Let the counterweights be removed,' Mr Platnauer translates with a straightforwardness of language that does less than justice to the syntactical extravagances of the original, 'and let the mobile crane descend, lowering on to the lofty stage men who, wheeling chorus-wise, scatter flames. Let Vulcan forge balls of fire to roll innocuously across the boards. Let the flames appear to play about the sham beams of the scenery and a tame conflagration, never allowed to rest, wander among the untouched towers.'

After the fall of Rome, pyrotechny became, once more, exclusively a military art. Its greatest triumph was the invention by Callinicus, about A.D. 650, of the famous Greek Fire – the secret weapon which enabled a dwindling Byzantine Empire to hold out for so long against its enemies.

During the Renaissance fireworks re-entered the world of popular entertainment. With every advance in the science of chemistry, they became more and more brilliant. By the middle of the nineteenth century pyrotechny had reached a peak of technical perfection and was capable of transporting vast multitudes of spectators towards the visionary antipodes of minds which, consciously, were respectable Methodist, Puseyites, Utilitarians, disciples of Mill or Marx, of Newman, or Bradlaugh, or Samuel Smiles. In the Piazza del Popolo, at Ranelagh and the Crystal Palace, on every Fourth and Fourteenth of July, the popular sub-conscious was reminded by the crimson glare of strontium, by copper blue and barium green and sodium yellow, of that Other World, down under, in the psychological equivalent of Australia.

Pageantry is a visionary art which has been used, from time immemorial, as a political instrument. The gorgeous fancy dress worn by Kings, Popes and their respective retainers, military and ecclesiastical, has a very practical purpose – to impress the lower classes with a lively sense of their masters' superhuman greatness. By means of fine clothes and solemn ceremonies, *de facto* domination is transformed into a rule not merely *de jure*, but positively, *de jure divino*. The crowns and tiaras, the assorted jewellery, the satins, silks and velvets, the gaudy uniforms and vestments, the crosses and medals, the sword hilts and the croziers, the plumes in the cocked hats and their clerical equivalents, those huge feather fans which make every papal function look like a tableau from *Aida* – all these are vision-inducing properties, designed to make all too human gentlemen and ladies look like heroes, demigoddesses and seraphs, and giving, in the process, a great deal of innocent pleasure to all concerned, actors and spectators alike.

In the course of the last two hundred years the tech-nology of artificial lighting has made enormous pro-gress, and this progress has contributed very greatly to the effectiveness of pageantry and the closely related art of theatrical spectacle. The first notable advance was made in the eighteenth century, with the introduction of moulded spermaceti candles in place of the older tallow dip and poured wax taper. Next came the invention of Argand's tubular wick, with an air supply on the inner as well as the outer surface of the flame. Glass chimneys speedily followed, and it became possible, for the first time in history, to burn oil with a bright and completely smokeless light. Coal gas was first employed as an illuminant in the early years of the nineteenth century, and in 1825 Thomas Drummond found a practical way of heating lime to incandescence by means of an oxygen-hydrogen or oxygen-coal gas flame. Meanwhile parabolic reflectors for concentrating light into a narrow beam had come into use. (The first English lighthouse equipped with such a reflector was built in 1790.)

The influence on pageantry and theatrical spectacle of these inventions was profound. In earlier times civic and religious ceremonies could only take place during the day (and days were as often cloudy as fine), or by the light, after sunset, of smoky lamps and torches or the feeble twinkling of candles. Argand and Drummond, gas, limelight and, forty years later, electricity made it possible to evoke, from the boundless chaos of night, rich island universes, in which the glitter of metal and gems, the sumptuous glow of velvets and brocades were intensified to the highest pitch of what may be called intrinsic significance. A recent example of ancient pageantry, raised by twentieth-century lighting to a higher magical power, was the coronation of Queen Elizabeth II. In the motion picture of the event, a ritual of transporting splendour was saved from the oblivion which, up till now, has always been the fate of such solemnities, and preserved it, blazing praeter-naturally under the floodlights, for the delight of a vast contemporary and future audience.

Two distinct and separate arts are practised in the

theatre – the human art of the drama, and the visionary, other-world art of spectacle. Elements of the two arts may be combined in a single evening's entertainment – the drama being interrupted (as so often happens in elaborate productions of Shakespeare) to permit the audience to enjoy a *tableau vivant*, in which the actors either remain still or, if they move, move only in a non-dramatic way, ceremonially, processionally or in a formal dance. Our concern here is not with drama; it is with theatrical spectacle, which is simply pageantry without its political or religious overtones.

In the minor visionary arts of the costumier and the designer of stage jewellery our ancestors were consummate masters. Nor, for all their dependence on unassisted muscle power, were they far behind us in the building and working of stage machinery, the contrivance of 'special effects.' In the masques of Elizabethan and early Stuart times, divine descents and irruptions of demons from the cellarage were a commonplace; so were apocalypses, so were the most amazing metamorphoses. Enormous sums of money were lavished on these spectacles. The Inns of Court, for example, put on a show for Charles I which cost more than twenty thousand pounds – at a date when the purchasing power of the pound was six or seven times what it is to-day.

'Carpentry,' said Ben Jonson sarcastically, 'is the soul of masque.' His contempt was motivated by resentment. Inigo Jones was paid as much for designing the scenery as was Ben for writing the libretto. The outraged laureate had evidently failed to grasp the fact that masque is a visionary art, and that visionary experience is beyond words (at any rate beyond all but the most Shakespearean words) and is to be evoked by direct, unmediated perceptions of things that remind the beholder of what is going on at the unexplored antipodes of his own personal consciousness. The soul of masque could never, in the very nature of things, be a Jonsonian libretto; it *had* to be carpentry. But even carpentry could not be the masque's whole soul. When it comes to us from within, visionary experience is always praeternaturally brilliant. But the early set designers possessed no manageable illuminant brighter than a candle. At close range a candle can create the most magical lights and contrasting shadows. The visionary paintings of Rembrandt and Georges de Latour are of things and persons seen by candlelight. Unfortunately light obeys the law of the inverse squares. At a safe distance from an actor in inflammable fancy dress, candles are hopelessly inadequate. At ten feet, for example, it would take one hundred of the best wax tapers to produce an effective illumination of one foot-candle. With such miserable lighting only a fraction of the masque's visionary potentialities could be made actual. Indeed, its visionary potentialities were not fully realized until long after it had ceased, in its original form, to exist. It was only in the nineteenth century, when advancing technology had equipped the theatre with limelight and parabolic reflectors, that the masque came fully into its own. Victoria's reign was the heroic age of the so-called Christmas pantomime and the fantastic spectacle. 'Ali Baba,' 'The King of the Peacocks,' 'The Golden Branch,' 'The Island of Jewels' – their very names are magical. The soul of that theatrical magic was carpentry and dressmaking; its indwelling spirit, its *scintilla animae*, was gas and limelight and, after the 'eighties, electricity. For the first time in the history of the stage, beams of brightest incandescence transfigured the painted backdrops, the costumes, the glass and pinchbeck of jewellery, so that they became capable of transporting the spectators towards that Other World which lies at the back of every mind, however perfect its adaptation to the exigencies of social life – even the social life of Mid-Victorian England. Today we are in the fortunate position of being able to squander half a million horsepower on the nightly illumination of a metropolis. And yet, in spite of this devaluation of artificial light, theatrical spectacle still retains its old compelling magic. Embodied in ballets, revues and musical comedies, the soul of masque goes marching along. Thousand-watt lamps and parabolic reflectors project beams of praeternatural light, and praeternatural light evokes, in everything it touches, praeternatural colour and praeternatural significance. Even the silliest spectacle can be rather wonderful. It is a case of a New World having been called in to redress the balance of the old – of visionary art making up for the deficiencies of all too human drama.

Athanasius Kircher's invention – if his, indeed, it was – was christened from the first *Lanterna Magica*. The name was everywhere adopted as perfectly appropriate to a machine, whose raw material was light, and whose finished product was a coloured image emerging from the darkness. To make the original magic lantern show yet more magical, Kircher's successors devised a number of methods for imparting life and movement to the projected image. There were 'chromatropic' slides, in which two painted glass discs could be made to revolve in opposite directions, producing a crude but still effective imitation of those perpetually changing three-dimensional patterns, which have been seen by virtually everyone who has had a vision, whether spontaneous or induced by drugs, fasting or the stroboscopic lamp. Then there were those 'dissolving views,' which reminded the spectator of the metamorphoses going on incessantly at the antipodes of his everyday consciousness. To make one scene turn imperceptibly into another, two magic lanterns were used, projecting coincident images on the screen. Each lantern was fitted with a shutter, so arranged that the light of one could be progressively dimmed, while the light of the other (originally completely obscured) was progressively brightened. In this way the view projected by the first lantern was insensibly replaced by the view by the second – to the delight and astonishment of all beholders. Another device was the mobile magic lantern, projecting its image on a semi-transparent screen, on the further side of which sat the audience. When the lantern was wheeled close to the screen, the projected image was very small. As it was withdrawn, the image became progressively larger. An automatic focussing device kept the changing images sharp and unblurred at all distances. The word 'phantasmagoria' was coined in 1802 by the inventors of this new kind of peepshow.

All these improvements in the technology of magic lanterns were contemporary with the poets and painters of the Romantic Revival, and may perhaps have exercised a certain influence on their choice of subject-matter and their methods of treating it. *Queen Mab* and *The Revolt of Islam*, for example, are full of Dissolving Views and Phantasmagorias. Keats's descriptions of scenes and persons, of interiors and furniture and effects of light, have the intense beamy quality of coloured images on a white sheet in a darkened room. John

Martin's representations of Satan and Belshazzar, of Hell and Babylon and the Deluge, are manifestly inspired by lantern slides and *tableaux vivants* dramatically illuminated by limelight.

The twentieth-century equivalent of the magic lantern show is the coloured movie. In the huge, expensive 'spectaculars,' the soul of masque goes marching along – with a vengeance sometimes, but sometimes also with taste and a real feeling for vision-inducing phantasy. Moreover, thanks to advancing technology, the coloured documentary has proved itself, in skilful hands, a notable new form of popular visionary art. The immensely magnified cactus blossoms, into which, at the end of Disney's *The Living Desert*, the spectator finds himself sinking, come straight from the Other World. And then what transporting visions, in the best of the nature films, of foliage in the wind, of the textures of rock and sand, of the shadows and emerald lights in grass or among the reeds, of birds and insects and four-footed creatures going about their business in the underbrush or among the branches of forest trees! Here are the magical close-up landscapes which fascinated the makers of *mille-feuille* tapestries, the mediaeval painters of gardens and hunting scenes. Here are the enlarged and isolated details of living nature out of which the artists of the Far East made some of the most beautiful of their paintings.

And then there is what may be called the Distorted Documentary – a strange new form of visionary art, admirably exemplified by Mr Francis Thompson's film, 'NY, NY.' In this very strange and beautiful picture we see the city of New York as it appears when photographed through multiplying prisms, or reflected in the backs of spoons. polished hub caps, spherical and parabolic mirrors. We still recognize houses, people, shop fronts, taxi cabs, but recognize them as elements in one of those living geometries which are so characteristic of the visionary experience. The invention of this new cinematographic art seems to presage (thank heaven!) the supersession and early demise of non-representational painting. It is used to be said by the non-representationalists that coloured photography had reduced the old-fashioned portrait and the old-fashioned landscape to the rank of otiose absurdities. This, of course, is completely untrue. Coloured photography merely records and preserves, in an easily reproducible form, the raw materials with which portraitists and landscape painters work. Used as Mr Thompson has used it, coloured cinematography does much more than merely record and preserve the raw materials of non-representational art; it actually turns out the finished product. Looking at 'NY, NY,' I was amazed to see that virtually every pictorial device invented by the Old Masters of non-representational art and reproduced *ad nauseam* by the academicians and mannerists of the school, for the last forty years or more, makes its appearance, alive, glowing, intensely significant, in the sequences of Mr Thompson's film.

Our ability to project a powerful beam of light has not only enabled us to create new forms of visionary art; it has also endowed one of the most ancient arts, the art of sculpture, with a new visionary quality which it did not previously possess. I have spoken in an earlier paragraph of the magical effects produced by the flood-lighting of ancient monuments and natural objects. Analogous effects are seen when we turn the spotlights on to sculptured stone. Fuseli got the inspiration from some of his best and wildest pictorial ideas by studying the statues on Monte Cavallo by the light of the setting sun, or, better still, when illuminated by lightning flashes at midnight. Today we dispose of artificial sunsets and synthetic lightning. We can illuminate our statues from whatever angle we choose, and with practically any desired degree of intensity. Sculpture, in consequence, has revealed fresh meanings and unsuspected beauties. Visit the Louvre one night, when the Greek and Egyptian antiquities are floodlit. You will meet with new gods, nymphs and Pharaohs, you will make the acquaintance, as one spotlight goes out and another, in a different quarter of space, is lit up, of a whole family of unfamiliar Victories of Samothrace.

The past is not something fixed and unalterable. Its facts are re-discovered by every succeeding generation, its values re-assessed, its meanings re-defined in the context of present tastes and preoccupations. Out of the same documents and monuments and works of art, every epoch invents its own Middle Ages, its private China, its patented and copyrighted Hellas. Today, thanks to recent advances in the technology of lighting, we can go one further than our predecessors. Not only have we reinterpreted the great works of sculpture bequeathed to us by the past; we have actually succeeded in altering the physical appearance of these works. Greek statues, as we see them illuminated by a light that never was on land or sea, and then photographed in a series of fragmentary close-ups from the oddest angles, bear almost no resemblance to the Greek statues seen by art critics and the general public in the dim galleries and decorous engravings of the past. The aim of the classical artist, in whatever period he may happen to live, is to impart order to the chaos of experience, to present a comprehensible, rational picture of reality in which all the parts are clearly seen and coherently related, so that the beholder knows (or, to be more accurate, imagines that he knows) precisely what's what. To us this ideal of rational orderliness makes no appeal. Consequently, when we are confronted by works of classical art, we use all the means in our power to make them look like something which they are not, and were never meant to be. From a work, whose whole point is its unity of conception, we select a single feature, focus our searchlights upon it and so force it, out of all context, upon the observer's consciousness. Where a contour seems to us too continuous, too obviously comprehensible, we break it up by alternating impenetrable shadows with patches of glaring brightness. When we photograph a sculptured figure or group, we use the camera to isolate a part which we then exhibit in enigmatic independence from the whole. By such means we can de-classicize the severest classic. Subjected to the light treatment and photographed by an expert camera man, a Pheidias becomes a piece of Gothic expressionism, a Praxiteles is turned into a fascinating *surréaliste* object dredged up from the ooziest depths of the subconscious. This may be bad art history, but it is certainly enormous fun.

Appendix IV

Painter in ordinary first to the Duke of his native Lorraine and later to the King of France, Georges de Latour was treated, during his lifetime, as the great artist he so manifestly was. With the accession of Louis XIV and the rise, the deliberate cultivation, of a new Art of Versailles, aristocratic in subject-matter and lucidly classical in style, the reputation of this once famous man suffered an eclipse so complete that, within a couple of generations, his very name had been forgotten, and his surviving paintings came to be attributed to the Le Nains, to Honthorst, to Zurbaran, to Murillo, even to Velasquez. The rediscovery of Latour began in 1915 and was virtually complete by 1934, when the Louvre organized a notable exhibition of 'The Painters of Reality.' Ignored for nearly three hundred years, one of the greatest of French painters had come back to claim his rights.

Georges de Latour was one of those extroverted visionaries, whose art faithfully reflects certain aspects of the outer world, but reflects them in a state of transfiguration, so that every meanest particular becomes intrinsically significant, a manifestation of the absolute. Most of his compositions are of figures seen by the light of a single candle. A single candle, as Caravaggio and the Spaniards had shown, can give rise to the most enormous theatrical effects. But Latour took no interest in theatrical effects. There is nothing dramatic in his pictures, nothing tragic or pathetic or grotesque, no representation of action, no appeal to the sort of emotions which people go to the theatre to have excited and then appeased. His personages are essentially static. They never *do* anything; they are simply *there* in the same way in which a granite Pharaoh is there, or a Bodhisattva from Khmer, or one of Piero's flat-footed angels. And the single candle is used, in every case, to stress this intense but unexcited, impersonal thereness. By exhibiting common things in an uncommon light, its flame makes manifest the living mystery and inexplicable marvel of mere existence. There is so little religiosity in the paintings that in many cases it is impossible to decide whether we are confronted by an illustration to the Bible or a study of models by candlelight. Is the 'Nativity' at Rennes *the* nativity, or merely *a* nativity? Is the picture of an old man asleep under the eyes of a young girl merely that? Or is it of St Peter in prison being visited by the delivering angel? There is no way of telling. But though Latour's art is wholly without religiosity, it remains profoundly religious, in the sense that it reveals, with unexampled intensity, the divine omnipresence.

It must be added that, as a man, this great painter of God's immanence seems to have been proud, hard, intolerably overbearing and avaricious. Which goes to show, yet once more, that there is never a one-to-one correspondence between an artist's work and his character.

Appendix V

At the near-point Vuillard painted interiors for the
most part, but sometimes also gardens. In a few compositions he managed to combine the magic of propinquity with the magic of remoteness by representing
a corner of a room, in which there stands or hangs one
of his own, or someone else's, representation of a distant
view of trees, hills and sky. It is an invitation to make
the best of both worlds, the telescopic and the micro-
scopic, at a single glance.

For the rest, I can think of only a very few close-up
landscapes by modern European artists. There is a
strange 'Thicket' by Van Gogh at the Metropolitan.
There is Constable's wonderful 'Dell in Helmingham
Park' at the Tate. There is a bad picture, Millais'
'Ophelia,' made magical, in spite of everything, by its
intricacies of summer greenery seen from the point of
view, very nearly, of a water rat. And I remember a
Delacroix, glimpsed long ago at some Loan Exhibition,
of bark and leaves and blossom at the closest range.
There must, of course, be others; but either I have
forgotten, or have never seen them. In any case there is
nothing in the West comparable to the Chinese and
Japanese renderings of nature at the near-point. A
spray of blossoming plum, eighteen inches of bamboo
stem with its leaves, tits or finches seen at hardly more
than arm's length among the bushes, all kinds of
flowers and foliage, of birds and fish and small mammals.
Each small life is represented as the centre of its own
universe, the purpose, in its own estimation, for which

this world and all that is in it were created; each issues its own specific and individual declaration of independence from human imperialism; each, by ironic implication, derides our absurd pretensions to lay down merely human rules for the conduct of the cosmic game; each mutely repeats the divine tautology: I am that I am.

Nature at the middle distance is familiar – so familiar that we are deluded into believing that we really know what it is all about. Seen very close at hand, or at a great distance, or from an odd angle, it seems disquietingly strange, wonderful beyond all comprehension. The close-up landscapes of China and Japan are so many illustrations of the theme that Samsara and Nirvana are one, that the Absolute is manifest in every appearance. These great metaphysical, and yet pragmatic, truths were rendered by the Zen-inspired artists of the Far East in yet another way. All the objects of their near-point scrutiny were represented in a state of unrelatedness, against a blank of virgin silk or paper. Thus isolated, these transient appearances take on a kind of absolute Thing-in-Itselfhood. Western artists have used this device when painting sacred figures, portraits and, sometimes, natural objects at a distance. Rembrandt's 'Mill' and Van Gogh's 'Cypresses' are examples of long-range landscapes, in which a single feature has been absolutized by isolation. The magical power of many of Goya's etchings, drawings and paintings can be accounted for by the fact that his compositions almost always take the form of a few silhouettes, or even a single silhouette, seen against a blank. These silhouetted shapes possess the visionary quality of intrinsic significance, heightened by isolation and unrelatedness to praeternatural intensity.

In nature, as in a work of art, the isolation of an

object tends to invest it with absoluteness, to endow it with that more-than-symbolic meaning which is identical with being.

> *But there's a tree – of many, one –*
> *A single field which I have looked upon:*
> *Both of them speak of something that is gone.*

The something which Wordsworth could no longer see was 'the visionary gleam.' That gleam, I remember, and that intrinsic significance were the properties of a solitary oak that could be seen from the train, between Reading and Oxford, growing from the summit of a little knoll in a wide expanse of ploughland, and silhouetted against the pale northern sky.

The effects of isolation combined with proximity may be studied, in all their magical strangeness, in an extraordinary painting by a seventeenth-century Japanese artist, who was also a famous swordsman and a student of Zen. It represents a butcher bird, perched on the very tip of a naked branch, 'waiting without purpose, but in the state of highest tension.' Beneath, above and all around is nothing. The bird emerges from the Void, from that eternal namelessness and formlessness, which is yet the very substance of the manifold, concrete and transient universe. That shrike on its bare branch is first cousin to Hardy's wintry thrush. But whereas the Victorian thrush insists on teaching us some kind of a lesson, the Far Eastern butcher bird is content simply to exist, to be intensely and absolutely *there*.

Appendix VI

Many schizophrenics pass most of their time neither on earth, nor in heaven, nor even in hell, but in a grey, shadowy world of phantoms and unrealities. What is true of these psychotics is true, to a lesser extent, of certain neurotics afflicted by a milder form of mental illness. Recently it has been found possible to induce this state of ghostly existence by administering a small quantity of one of the derivatives of adrenalin. For the living, the doors of heaven, hell and limbo are opened, not by 'massy keys of metals twain,' but by the presence in the blood of one set of chemical compounds and the absence of another set. The shadow-world inhabited by some schizophrenics and neurotics closely resembles the world of the dead, as described in some of the earlier religious traditions. Like the wraiths in Sheol and in Homer's Hades, these mentally disturbed persons have lost touch with matter, language and their fellow beings. They have no purchase on life and are condemned to ineffectiveness, solitude and a silence broken only by the senseless squeak and gibber of ghosts.

The history of eschatological ideas marks a genuine progress – a progress which can be described in theological terms as the passage from Hades to Heaven, in chemical terms as the substitution of mescalin and lysergic acid for adrenolutin, and in psychological terms as the advance from catatonia and feelings of unreality to a sense of heightened reality in vision and, finally, in mystical experience.

Appendix VII

Géricault was a negative visionary; for though his art was almost obsessively true to nature, it was true to a nature that had been magically transfigured, in his perceiving and rendering of it, for the worse. 'I start to paint a woman,' he once said, 'but it always ends up as a lion.' More often, indeed, it ended up as something a good deal less amiable than a lion – as a corpse, for example, or as a demon. His masterpiece, the prodigious 'Raft of the *Medusa*,' was painted not from life but from dissolution and decay – from bits of cadavers supplied by medical students, from the emaciated torso and jaundiced face of a friend who was suffering from a disease of the liver. Even the waves on which the raft is floating, even the overarching sky are corpse-coloured. It is as though the entire universe had become a dissecting room.

And then there are his demonic pictures. 'The Derby,' it is obvious, is being run in hell, against a background fairly blazing with darkness visible. 'The Horse startled by Lightning,' in the National Gallery, is the revelation, in a single frozen instant, of the strangeness, the sinister and even infernal otherness that hides in familiar things. In the Metropolitan Museum there is a portrait of a child. And what a child! In his luridly brilliant jacket the little darling is what Baudelaire liked to call 'a budding Satan,' *un Satan en herbe*. And the study of a naked man, also in the Metropolitan, is none other than the budding Satan grown up.

From the accounts which his friends have left of him it is evident that Géricault habitually saw the world about him as a succession of visionary apocalypses. The prancing horse of his early *Officier de Chasseurs* was seen one morning, on the road to Saint-Cloud, in a dusty glare of summer sunshine, rearing and plunging between the shafts of an omnibus. The personages in the 'Raft of the *Medusa*' were painted in finished detail, one by one, on the virgin canvas. There was no outline drawing of the whole composition, no gradual building up of an over-all harmony of tones and hues. Each particular revelation – of a body in decay, of a sick man in the ghastly extremity of hepatitis – was fully rendered as it was seen and artistically realized. By a miracle of genius, every successive apocalypse was made to fit, prophetically, into a harmonious composition which existed, when the first of the appalling visions was transferred to canvas, only in the artist's imagination.

Appendix VIII

In *Sartor Resartus* Carlyle has left what (in *Mr Carlyle, my Patient*) his psycho-somatic biographer, Dr James Halliday, calls 'an amazing description of a psychotic state of mind, largely depressive, but partly schizophrenic.'

'The men and women around me,' writes Carlyle, 'even speaking with me, were but Figures; I had practically forgotten that they were alive, that they were not merely automata. Friendship was but an incredible tradition. In the midst of their crowded streets and assemblages I walked solitary; and (except that it was my own heart, not another's, that I kept devouring) savage also as the tiger in the jungle. ... To me the Universe was all void of Life, of Purpose, of Volition, even of Hostility; it was one huge, dead immeasurable steam-engine, rolling on in its dead indifference, to grind me limb from limb. ... Having no hope, neither had I any definite fear, were it of Man or of Devil. And yet, strangely enough, I lived in a continual, indefinite, pining fear, tremulous, pusillanimous, apprehensive of I knew not what; it seemed as if all things in the Heavens above and the Earth beneath, would hurt me; as if the Heavens and the Earth were but the boundless jaws of a devouring Monster, wherein I, palpitating, waited to be devoured.' Renée and the idolater of heroes are evidently describing the same experience. Infinity is apprehended by both, but in the form of 'the System,' the 'immeasurable Steam-Engine.' To both, again, all is significant, but negatively significant, so that every event is utterly pointless, every object intensely unreal, every self-styled human being a clockwork dummy, grotesquely going through the motions of work and play, of loving, hating, thinking, of being eloquent, heroic, saintly, what you will – the robots are nothing if not versatile.

Aldous Huxley

The Human Situation

With a Foreword by Steve Jones

'*The Human Situation* is beautifully written, full of sidelights and quotations which magnificently illuminate the subjects.'   *Listener*

Prophet, mystic, wit, satirist, man of science – the many sides of Huxley's all-encompassing intellect are on abundant display in this series of lectures given in 1959, four years before his death. Huxley's aim was to bring together a number of themes and disciplines – human biology, the state of the planet, society and politics, the individual and his capabilities – to present a complete prospectus of the human condition, highlighting the major problems facing mankind if it is to survive into the 21st century. Wise, passionate and chillingly prescient, *The Human Situation* reminds us why Huxley is one of the most important thinkers of our time.

'Huxley was a bridge builder, whose mind stretches across the gap between art and science. In *The Human Situation*, Huxley's efforts to fabricate a world order from his own intelligence are full of mental virtuosity and resourceful optimism.'   *New Statesman*

Aldous Huxley

Crome Yellow

With an Introduction by Malcolm Bradbury

'Delightful. *Crome Yellow* is witty, wordly and poetic.' *The Times*

Denis Stone, a tender young poet, is invited to spend the weekend in the rarefied atmosphere of Crome, renowned for its gatherings of 'bright young things'. Hosted by the world-weary Henry Wimbush and his exotic wife Priscilla, the weekend has much to offer the ingenuous and excitable Denis. From the flaxen-haired Mary Bracegirdle, a student of psychoanalysis, to the ravishing, raven-haired Misses Lapith, the possibilities for romantic intrigue are endless. But just below the witty, glittering surface lurk distinctly sinister and ignoble motives, destined to bring the starry-eyed Denis back to earth with a nasty bump.

First published in 1921, *Crome Yellow* was Aldous Huxley's much-acclaimed debut novel. With the evident relish of the true satirist, he mocked the fads, foibles and spirit of his time with an unsurpassed wit and brilliance. The Twenties have never been better represented – or more entertainingly dismissed.

'With a strong, delightful and admirable talent for caricature, Huxley is at his entertaining best in his grimaces at modern movements and at the ridiculous earnestness of the young.'

Observer

Aldous Huxley

Island

With an Introduction by David Bradshaw

'In the whole history of world literature, no writer has been better equipped to create images of false and true utopias than Aldous Huxley. Even when he has been satirizing the false, the true has always been implicit in his work. We cannot deny *Island*'s brilliance, its learning and its honest attempt to answer the big human questions.'
Anthony Burgess

For over a hundred years the Pacific island of Pala has been the scene of a unique experiment in civilization. At the instigation of a Scottish doctor and a Buddhist king, western science has been brought together with the philosophy and humanism of the East, making the island community a paradise on earth. When Will Farnaby, a cynical, disillusioned journalist, arrives in their midst on an undisclosed search for information about Pala's massive unexploited oil reserves, he is taken wholeheartedly under the islanders' wing. Drawn ever further into their trust, he becomes convinced that this extraordinary way of life should remain unspoilt. Soon, the need to complete his mission becomes an intolerable burden . . .

If *Brave New World* is Huxley's glimpse into hell, then *Island* is his vision of utopia. In this, his last novel, mankind is portrayed at its sanest and most admirable.

'*Island*'s theme is integration and Huxley uses this with disconcerting brilliance. The familiar coruscation of his writing is shown here at its best.'
Guardian

Aldous Huxley

Eyeless in Gaza

With an Introduction by David Bradshaw

'*Eyeless in Gaza* embodies Huxley's conclusions about life. Amusing, moving and brilliant, there is no doubting the sincerity and the beauty of this book.'
Listener

Anthony Beavis, a *dilettante* social theorist, is a man inclined to recoil from life. The pleasures of the physical world disgust him and the universe of ideas is but a poor refuge. Having long lost the art of intimacy, he betrays friendships and toys cruelly with the affections of women. But as Beavis approaches middle age, his world of perfect detachment begins to lose its appeal. Finally realising that his withdrawal from life has been motivated not by intellectual honesty but by moral cowardice, Beavis, devastated and at crisis point, meets the remarkable and redoubtable Dr Miller . . .

Eyeless in Gaza offers a counterpoint to the biting cynicism of Huxley's earlier satirical novels, and is considered by many to be his definitive work of fiction.

'In *Eyeless in Gaza*, the play of ideas and theories, moral, psychological and sociological, is profuse and scintillating.'
Times Literary Supplement

Aldous Huxley

The Perennial Philosophy

With an Introduction by David Bradshaw

'*The Perennial Philosophy* is a mine of curious and erudite learning. The running commentary is clear and vivid, and nobody reading it can fail to recognise that he is in the presence of a mind both profound and acute.'   *New Statesman*

There are at least ten different renderings in ten different sacred texts of the advice familiar to Christians as 'Do unto others as you would have them do unto you.' Does this mean that the revelations of mystics and the beliefs of the wise and holy of all ages, races and creeds can be distilled into a single set of unifying, transcendent truths?

Drawing on a vast range of sources – including the Ghita and the Upanishads, the Buddhist philosophers, the Taoists, the Sufis, the early Quakers and the great Catholic mystics of the Middle Ages, *The Perennial Philosophy* is Huxley's attempt to offer just such a synthesis for the enlightenment of the modern world.

'A rich and valuable anthology.'   *Spectator*

Aldous Huxley

Point Counter Point

With an Introduction by David Bradshaw

'Huxley's style is at once dry and rich, intellectual and sensuous, scholarly and romantic. *Point Counter Point* is extremely funny with passages of rich and gorgeous farce.'   *Observer*

In Twenties London, the writers, artists, wastrels and dilettantes who frequent Lady Edward Tantamount's Pall Mall parties are permanently engaged in pushing forward the moral frontiers of the age. Marjorie Carling has left her family to live with the writer, Walter Bidlake; the luscious but cold-hearted Lucy Tantamount is set on devouring every man in sight; the repulsive Spandrell insists on entertaining everyone with his accounts of how he debauches young girls; and even Lady Tantamount herself, long tired of her husband and his unwavering devotion to the study of newts, has taken a lover – the fashionable painter and expert taker of virginities, John Bidlake. Only Rampion is left to maintain standards of decency in this increasingly degenerate world . . .

Often described as a *Vanity Fair* for the Twenties. *Point Counter Point* contains wickedly accurate portraits of D. H. Lawrence, Katherine Mansfield, Ottoline Morrell and Huxley himself.

'As a piece of satire, often brilliant, sometimes wise, *Point Counter Point* is a monstrous exposure of a society which confuses pleasure with happiness, sensation with sensibility, mood with opinion, opinion with conviction and self with God.'   *Guardian*